Praise for

MY RADIO RADIO

"There are few contemporary novels that I truly admire. Van Eerden's novel rises to the top of my list."
—Margot Singer, author of *The Pale of Settlement*

"A book of surprises—surprises that emanate not so much from dramatic action but as a rich consequence of the crafting of character through language. Page after page, the reader is treated to beautifully cadenced, strikingly voiced observations and reflections that shape the poetic sensibility of the coming-of-age narrator, Omi Ruth. The reader reads and keeps reading for the wonder of Omi Ruth's utterances, for her quirky and tender insights."
—Karen Brennan, author of *little dark* and *Monsters*

"It's rare to fall for a voice, to want nothing more than just to listen. So I finished Jessie van Eerden's *My Radio Radio* feeling something like grief, lovelorn, my heart captive to the voice of Omi Ruth, a girl who sees the world so fresh she makes it new."
—Kevin Oderman, author of *White Vespa*
and *Cannot Stay: Essays on Travel*

"Reading *My Radio Radio* is like swimming under the luminous skin of life, above us ghostly insights come and go, below us the deep unknown threatens, and then we poke through pores of enlightenment and recognize things hidden since the foundation of the world. Jessie van Eerden is a writer that makes it seem the rest of us are merely scratching the surface."
—Richard Schmitt, author of *The Aerialist*

"*My Radio Radio* will tune you in from the beginning and leave you wanting more by the end. Jessie van Eerden is at her tender and lyrical best in this story of longing and belonging. Her young narrator, Naomi Ruth, is a kissing cousin to Ellen Foster but finally in a league and family of her own. Welcome her with open arms."

—Paul J. Willis, author of *The Alpine Tales*

MY RADIO RADIO

a novel

Jessie van Eerden

VANDALIA PRESS • MORGANTOWN • 2016

Vandalia Press / An imprint of West Virginia University Press

Copyright 2016 Jessie van Eerden

All rights reserved

First edition published 2016 by Vandalia Press

Printed in the United States of America

ISBN:

paper: 978-1-943665-08-2

epub: 978-1-943665-09-9

pdf: 978-1-943665-10-5

Library of Congress Cataloging-in-Publication Data

is available from the Library of Congress

Book and cover design by Than Saffel. Cover photograph by Korri Crowley.

for my sisters, Michaelanne & Diane

CONTENTS

FINDING NORTH

I WOKE up too fast, that's all. I swung my feet to the floor and upset some bowl inside me, and whatever happened inside must have happened outside me, too. I think on it now with Clear Morning Mind. I've never thought so clearly, it's like I'm looking at a picture and the air gets so thin between me and it, that I climb inside the scene. "Strange child," I hear someone say real quietly and far away. It's Jude, I think, but it's not him I'm watching now. I'm slowing down time, I'm watching this picture of the morning hours just past, so clear it hurts. Why does it hurt, I'm trying to figure.

When I woke in a rush, the only sound was my feet slapping the floorboards, till I heard, out the window, the horse hooves and the buggy coming by with egg delivery. I thought it was an old time, for a minute or two, without cars and things. Then Vaughn Buey took the corner in his muscle car, those exhaust pipes like an awful belch. No, I knew then, it's not the old days. It's Indiana and it's 5 a.m. because that's when the Amish boy, Spencer Frye, puts the eggs on the back steps— and sometimes a flower in a jar of water—and takes the dollar left under the brick. And that's when Vaughn Buey comes off shift at the RV plant.

But I wasn't so awake to these things then like I am now as I stand here somehow far away from myself. I didn't have the Clear Morning Mind. It was more like dreaming, or hearing things say themselves inside my head, because all I thought about was the trickle I felt when I tipped over the bowl inside me and blood sneaked out between my legs.

"Oh no," I said out loud. That was the only noise then, my voice, sounding strange, like something played back to me on a tape. Then quiet. So quiet I could almost hear the blood dripping out of me. I listened for it like for rain going down the sidewalk drain after a storm. I couldn't see in the dark, but I knew on my nightgown there was a red spot, gone through my underwear. Nancy Calhoun says a stain happens sometimes when you're unprepared. She came again to the home school just last week, brought her two grandnieces and a trunk suitcase, first pulling out a sewing kit to make me think it was another sewing class. Then she brought out the plastic woman's womb. I'm twelve, nearly thirteen, and I thought the two girls were too young to be hearing about it. Maybe Nancy thought I'd be less embarrassed with them present, since I'm alone in the home school. Sue Calhoun teaches me all the subjects but home economics, which includes sewing steps and sex talk. Nancy doesn't live here in this big house with the seven of us, so no one wanted her teaching me sex and menstruation, but she's the only one who will do it. She drives all the way from her midwife clinic in South Bend to give me the talks. Even though she thinks our fellowship is a cult, she sweeps in and hugs me into the sleeves of her flowy blouses and says the only hope is the children.

Nancy did her job, and just in time. I knew right away this trickle was the first shedding from the bloody walls of my womb, like paint flowing down off the walls of my bedroom that is really just a big closet. I sat and pictured that in the dark: the paint dripping down the walls, each wall I'd painted a different pretty color. But I knew, around the dim outline of my single window, the blue paint was chipping into pieces and did not flow at all, so I quit that picture. I imagined a leaky tap instead, since that's what it felt like. Now there would be eggs coming each month. I pictured a tap with pretty brass fixtures at the sink, because our sinks are all rusted and gray, and just then it came faster. Somebody switched the tap on.

"Ooh," I said.

If I hadn't woken up so fast and slapped my feet so hard to the floorboards, I might have put off the blood, and my life might have been different. Everything might have been different. Maybe I would not have grown this sudden hunger for a hush to come over me and wrap me into it. I would not have starved so for this white white stillness that has started growing and spreading out like fog.

But I woke up too early and too fast, when everyone in Solomon's Porch still slept like stones on the creek-bottom of dreams. I sat in my own blood. It was for sure on the sheets now and not only on my gown, so what I did—as the youngest member of the Common Purse who had just turned into a grown woman by the switching on of the tap—what I did was run. Maybe I was trying to outrun my own blood, or run so the air would rush up between my legs and cool the blood and dry it. I ran out of my room into the wide hallway.

Right now, with time slowed down, I think this big house is funny, Solomon's Porch of the Common Purse—C.P. I call it. Funny because it's not a porch at all, in fact it's only got a tiny front stoop. It used to be a hotel, nothing fancy, especially the bathroom sinks with ugly fixtures, and the white walls everywhere, which are why I painted my room four colors. But it does have a tall pretty window with a stained-glass star at one end of the upstairs hallway. I'd like to bust up the three colors of glass for my mosaic wall out back, but really I could never smash it. It was so early, it was still dark out, but the sun was trying hard to get in through the window, and I ran toward it. The banister goes along the hall to bar the stairwell, and I see myself in slow motion now, as I reached out and caught my hand on one of the spindles to stop me short, the way the Buey boys do each other in a clothesline, so hard they can't breathe after. I was gentler than them, but I stopped cold and ran back to the right because, even with my thoughts foggy, I did remember my own rule— that when people are asleep, I don't go near the three bedroom doors down that hallway in front of the tall pretty window with the six-legged star. In those rooms, people sleep like the dead. People like Morse and Sue Calhoun when I passed that way one night, when their door stood open a crack. First door was shut. Second door was shut. Third door, open a smidge, and everyone was asleep but me, and probably my brother Wood listening to the radio in his room downstairs and Jude, too, in his straight-backed chair in the kitchen, reading Scripture and poems with his blue eyes full of tears. I tiptoed and peeked in at the two of them, and I knew it was only the Calhouns, but I couldn't see their faces. All I saw was bodies, his in underpants and hers in a nylon slip, no blankets because it was hot, and her arm was slung over his belly.

Dead, I thought, like the magazine pictures. For I look through *National Geographic* and *The Macedonian Call* missionary magazine every day—I tell them it's because I want to see all the foreign places and people Jesus has in mind to save. But really I want to cut out pictures for collages, and whether I cut and paste them or not, my mind holds all the pictures I see like a deep freezer—the C.P. people say I have a photographic memory, and I wonder. As I peeked in on the Calhouns, I saw the picture in *The Call*, a whole field of dead black bodies. One picture had a black boy alive in the field, he seemed the only boy alive in the world, his arms wide apart, like trying to catch a bride bouquet. And one close-up picture of a dead boy with his arm slung over another dead body, both bloody. So my freezer-mind opened up in the Calhouns' doorway, and that's what I saw in their room. A field full of the dead who God had not protected and Jesus might not have had the chance to save. I waited something like ten minutes to see Sue move her arm. I don't think I breathed. She never did move, so I went to my room and lay awake forever. Except not forever, because I slept through breakfast the next day, and who would come to check on me but Sue Calhoun dressed clean and bright, like a ghost. She had on the peach dress she often wore for the home school and she put her ghostly hand on my forehead, but I drew back. She gave me a cold bowl of Cream of Wheat and said a prayer over me. "Lord, might she come out of her shell," she prayed. They are always asking God might I come out of my shell.

So I don't pass by those doors anymore when people are asleep. This morning I ran the other way, past the bathroom and around the loop of banister. I don't know what I was think-ing—I don't guess I was thinking at all, nothing but fog and confusion, though I knew from Nancy's plastic woman where the tampon goes like a fat pencil, or the Always pad in your underwear. I knew she had put some of each under the bath-room sink we all shared. I'm smart, but I wasn't thinking at all. Things said themselves in my head, and "run" was the loudest thing that said itself. So I ran like a scared cat, and there I went in the morning darkness, racing around the banister into the corner room I thought to be empty. That said itself in my head, too—"Go ahead into that room."

The door was not locked since we never lock any doors. The Bible says to be open to the stranger at all times, it could be an angel wanting in to be waited on, it could be you're entertaining angels unawares. I turned the old crystal knob—the only other thing that's pretty in Solomon's Porch. The doorknobs, the four colors of my room's walls, and the starry window. I ran in and shut the door behind me.

And I expected to be alone. It was a room free to rent—in some ways, the C.P. house is turning itself back into a hotel since there are so few of us living here now. No one was renting that I knew of, no one ever rented. But right away, even in the darkness, I knew someone was there.

"Okay," I said, "okay," like I was calming a rowdy dog, but it was me I was calming and the someone in the room in case I'd caused a stir by barging in. I stood still and listened, letting my eyes get used to things. I heard an odd machine noise. *Click whirr, click whirr*, it went. Then, *hiss hmm, hiss hmm.*

The bed for renters was gone from the corner, or the mattress was gone and the collapsed steel frame leaned against the wall by the window. I turned toward the other window, and my eyes settled into seeing. Just under the hem of the curtains, I saw a man lying in a narrow bed with a railing.

"Okay," I said, "okay."

The *click* and *hiss* sounds came from the floor beside the man, a machine with a blinking red light. I stepped closer to him since he stayed still. My brother Wood and me, we're the kind that people call backward, inside a shell like a hermit crab, crawling out for only each other, so I don't know what made me so bold right then. Except that I'd just turned into a woman, and there was no way to reverse the effects that would happen to me now. My mind finally started clearing away the fog, and I had many thoughts at once, like I was trying to make up for not thinking earlier. I thought I should have run into the bathroom and taken care of things. I thought of the Amish buggy and Spencer Frye, the Amish boy who left the one-dollar dozen of eggs and the flower he leaves without saying who for. I thought of how the Amish must wish they could reverse time so cars wouldn't honk and hassle them. I thought of how Vaughn Buey was off shift and home next door and how he took girls for a ride and how the girls' hair flowed in easy waves with the windows down, and how I would need to learn to make waves with my stubborn curls that refused to spiral in a pretty way—for my hair is a thicket and one time Wood put a tiny rubber mouse in there when I slept, and it took me half a day to know it. I thought how I'd have to ask Nancy for a tube of lipstick now, as a woman, even though Wood thinks it makes a girl look like a clown. He never said so, but he didn't have to. I knew that's what he thought, like I knew mostly all his thoughts. We could be quiet together, he and I, at least we could before he went off to Bible college to learn broadcasting and started keeping secrets and left me alone to flip through the used-up books in the home school with Sue Calhoun who, for me, always stayed part ghost. Whenever Wood and I wanted, when he was still here in the C.P. house, we could make up live radio shows and record them on tape.

A thin tube ran from the machine to the man's nose, but it didn't seem to bother him. I got so close that even in the dim window light I could see some red chapping around his nostrils, and all the rest was white: his skin like it had no blood, his fine feather-hair that fanned onto his pillow, his sheets and blankets and nightshirt. His eyelids, too. A silent silver-white. I bent over him. "Okay," I said softly, like talking to a baby.

So little light came through the window, but light seemed to come up through his skin, like sun coming through the tree leaves so the veins are barely there, real faint. It was the prettiest thought I've ever had, and I wondered if it were a thought from God since God's thoughts are more beautiful and higher up than ours.

I felt a thin line of blood trail down my leg to my ankle and then my sole.

I could not outrun it.

"I guess you are the first to know me in this state," I said to the hushed man. I covered my mouth, "okay," then dropped my hand free to my side. I stayed looking in on him long enough for the blood to make a spot on the wooden floor. Silent silver-white. I stayed longer than I can say for sure, a long time, hours maybe—I've lost all track of time, and I'm tired. I don't remember sleeping, but I slept a little because I was on the floor when I finally heard noise downstairs. Everyone must be up, I thought, and I need to leave here before they catch me.

I rushed out like I had rushed in. I came around the banister loop and ran right into Jude, his skinny chest like a board hitting my face. My blood—I can't let him see it, I thought. He was crying, Jude was, but that was not uncommon for him. Then he took my shoulders in his hands and looked in my face.

"I'm so sorry," Jude said to me, his kind eyes so blue, like marbles, and his swept-back hair making him look always like a little boy even though he's thirty-something.

"Okay," I whispered. Did he know where I'd been?

"So sorry," he murmured again, and I thought, well, maybe he knows about the blood.

He held me and I held him back, awkwardly, like he needed it. His shoulder blades stuck out from his thin back. There was really nothing to be sorry about, every woman goes through it, but then, Jude might not know that as a celibate man. He leaned away from me and studied my face.

"They haven't told you, have they?" he said. "Oh, Sister Naomi." Jude cried without wiping his nose and snot ran into his mouth. "Sister Naomi. Your brother Wood is dead."

White white flash in my mind, clearing everything out. Everything.

"He was killed in a car wreck coming home. Sometime early this morning."

That takes me up to right now. Right here, where I am very still and heavy in my nightgown and in my blood by the banister in Jude's arms, outside time, or inside it. Thinking Clear Morning Thoughts, so clear it hurts. Jude says again, in his whisper, "Strange."

I say nothing for so long, even my mouth is white inside it. Then I say—out loud, I think, but I'm not sure—"I woke up too fast."

Jude holds me in his thin bony arms—he smells of chopped carrots, of bread. I will be careful to take my time waking up after today. I will sleep late and listen for people downstairs in the kitchen or in the hallway. When you wake up before everyone else, I guess you can trap them in their watery dreams. They can drown. Jude is saying, like he's telling me Wood's dream, "He was on his way home for summer break when a car hit head-on.

The other driver got out and Wood seemed okay, he walked away from the crash. Then he just fell over."

I picture Wood like a flower bending, too tall for its jar.

Here I am with no Wood. Just like that. Time slaps shut. All his radio voices he made up, all his secret thoughts. His eyes that are my eyes—we studied them one time in the mirror till our pupils got so wide they about cracked and spilled hazel eye color down our cheeks. I back away from Jude. His T-shirt collar is dark with tears, all his. I have shed none. That's what is strange. I back toward the corner room, my hand smoothing the banister as I go. I back up all the way to the door and put my hand on the old crystal knob. I ask, "Who is that man in there?"

"Sister Omi, you're in shock," says Jude to me, inching my way, careful.

"Who is he?" Like I'm standing guard outside this stranger's door, already caring for him. Like what my life will be behind this door will have to be for me to find out and Jude knows it and he can see that it will be full of dark and danger and lost-ness.

"That's Sister Loomis's North. Her law-husband Northrop. They brought him late last night from the nursing home to stay with us."

The sun is out full force now and strong, pouring its rays through the stained glass of the six-legged star around the corner. Jude's face is three colors at once, all shiny and wet. But the light doesn't reach where I am. And another drop of my womb's blood leaves me. The bright thick red leaves me.

QUIET TERRORS OF THE BODY

"My name is Naomi Ruth Wincott."

I say this to Loomis's North from a folding chair I found under the metal bed-frame parts and wooden slats leaning against the wall. My last collage sits under my chair to show him. It's the first time we've been alone today, no hospice nurse fussing. Two nurses alternate, one real sweet, one sour. The sweet one, Jayne, shows me how to do things, like change the bed, if I stand around long enough, and she does extra things that don't need doing, like pulling back his curtain in the daylight and sprinkling his sheets with cornstarch. The sour one shoos me like a housefly—Regina. She reminds me of Vaughn Buey's brother Odell laying block, real exact and hard. I asked Jayne—she's a real big lady—"Can he hear me?" And she said, "Yes, they can hear up till the end." The other said, "No, he's a vegetable." Regina has short hair plastered tight to her head; she's a stingy one, even with words. She fits in just fine here at the C.P., the Common Purse that never has enough in it to go around.

This is the first time I've spoken out loud to Loomis's North since I found him three days ago. The first words I've said to anybody, except the nurses because they don't know what has happened so they don't wrap me in pity like a cloth of pinpricks.

Out his window, I watch the power line wiggle under a bird over the alley. The bird can probably see all of Dunlap, Indiana, from up there since the town only goes for a couple miles before turning into cornfields, with a tall radio tower sticking up in the middle, far off. That bird could eye the fast food places, Cindy Lane's Diner, the bars I've never been to, the Kroger and hardware I have, and the RV plant and its warehouses taking up three blocks with concrete and metal. I look at the Bueys' house through the sheer curtains out the other window beside the long bed slats making a tall lean-to with the wall. Their house is brick and used to be part of the C.P., back when twenty-some families belonged to the fellowship, but the C.P. had to sell the house to Chastity Buey and her boys a few years after I was born. They sold the other house, too, the one across the alley I can't see from this room, with blue siding and red trim that makes it prettier than Solomon's Porch, which is all dirty white. The blue house is split into apartments that black people rent. I don't know anyone's name who lives in the apartments, but they're different ages: grown women, old women in scarves, and teen boys. I heard singing in there once like I've never heard anyplace else. One time Morse Calhoun called a meeting about locking our door that faces the apartments, on account of those boys. Morse has a mean flattop haircut, like he's in the army, and he acts like he is, too, like Leonard's second in command. He said he was putting his foot down, and nobody would say no, but then Jude started crying—maybe because of the angels wanting in—till Morse said, "Fine, leave it unlocked."

A walkway still runs through our backyard to the Bueys' backdoor. The curtains in this room are thin enough that I can see Vaughn's black shade is pulled down. He sleeps till evening since he's third shift at the plant. But he'll get up early today for the burial.

Feather-white of skin, cotton-puff hair. I can't think *burial* so I just see and see. I study the shining skin of Loomis's North. When I speak again, my voice has that played-back sound from a tape.

"Jayne says you can hear me and you could use the company. I thought I'd tell you some history about this place since it's uncommon. That's the funny word I use because it's Dunlap Fellowship of All Things in *Common*. The C.P. for short, for Common Purse, because we share all our money and are supposed to live like the first disciples of Jesus. And we call this house Solomon's Porch because, in the Book of Acts, that's the spot where the disciples gave a famous talk to all the world after healing a cripple."

I quit my speech, I sound too much like Leonard giving our history. I wish we had a real wraparound porch, a real swing to swing on alone. I think this old man and I would both like that today.

"My two names come from the Book of Ruth," I say, "which is my mother's favorite Bible book. It's a book that doesn't give you much on God, but it makes for a nice picture in the illustrated version—there's a pretty Ruth gathering barley sheaves. Carson is my mother, but we say 'law-mother, law-father' and use names. My law-father's Leonard, he's the one with the perfect-cut gray moustache and the one who calls the shots around here. There's supposed to be nothing special about family ties because we're all family according to Jesus. He said, 'Whoever does my will is my mother and brother.' There's no marriage in heaven either, Jesus said, so we get an early start on that rule and only get a little bit married here on earth. Law-husband, law-wife, like that. Carson and Leonard are married but you'd never know it. And we're supposed to say *Sister* Carson, but I don't say *sister* with the names. Nobody does but Jude."

I think to myself: and I don't say *brother*. I had one law-brother. And he's my only brother. I don't care what Jesus said. I had a brother named Woodrun Leonard Wincott Jr. and last time I saw him he had a secret close to him as a pillow, far away from him as a bird. I feel my throat closing, so I say, "Loomis is your law-wife, but you probably know that."

I think about old Loomis sleeping on the bottom floor in the room next to Jude. She is like a child but she's eighty-two, and here I am on the other end only twelve. Everyone else is in between—Jude, he's thirty-something, and my law-parents are forty-five and gray headed so they seem like old people, somehow older than this man lying here. I think how I feel old and how Jude lives downstairs like the hotel keep, sweeping up and cooking, and how Loomis is too weak to make the steps. I always thought, like Jude and like Nancy Calhoun, she wasn't married. Loomis is always nibbling on food and always clearing her throat, like she's full of sticky cobwebs that catch all the food and clog her up. Jude tells me her mind is failing, and I don't doubt it. I stay away from Loomis.

I look at this man's long slender left hand that I've not yet touched, milk colored, with a gold ring on his finger. It will never come off his knuckle, maybe not even in heaven. I guess he touched Loomis with that hand, stroked her hair, back when they both walked the world. Then I think: she can't make the steps to come up here and see her North. Why did she bring him here to the C.P.?

"So my name is Naomi Ruth," I tell him again. I say, "One time I looked in the Bible encyclopedia on Jude's shelves. Naomi means pleasant, my delight, and Ruth means friendship or beauty." This man can hear me and understand, I think. He'd understand how I took the encyclopedia to Leonard when he was working up a sermon for Christian radio, and I pointed to where it says Ruth means beauty. Leonard squinted, as if his perfect moustache itched him. "That refers to inward beauty," he said. "It means goodness." Then he went back to his sermon papers at the desk, turned his head the way he always does, like he's part machine. And I sank inside because I wanted to be beautiful instead of good. And I may have wanted him to stroke my beautiful cheek, saying, "Yes, just as pretty as that Ruth who was a queen misplaced in a barley field." But he only murmured into his papers that Ruth was faithful and obedient, like putting a black cloud over me. He used his sermon-voice too, which is a double-layer cake, one layer of kindness but the other of scorn. I took the encyclopedia back to my closet-room and read on. Ruth married some man who died and she stuck to that man's old law-mother, Naomi, like glue. Naomi had many losses, so she said, "Call me Mara," which means bitter. I thought that about myself, Call me Mara, because I wanted to be beautiful and knew I wasn't. I put the book back on Jude's shelf for Bibles and commentaries, above the shelf where he keeps volumes and volumes of poems. I touched their spines. I wanted my name in a poem, not a Bible encyclopedia.

"Let's see now," I say, because it feels better to talk than to not talk today. "So there's Jude who does the meals and the garden out back and reads Scripture all teary-eyed. There's Carson who I mentioned already, my law-mother. She's in correspondence school for nursing. Leonard I already told you is my law-father who bosses everybody, and he preaches and visits the lost and the sick and does his awful radio sermon on Sundays. Then Morse and Sue Calhoun whose law-daughter Lucy is gone, but I wear all her clothes secondhand. Sue teaches me home school, except for the things Nancy teaches—she's Morse's law-sister but she's not part of us. She's a midwife and what Leonard considers a godless woman. Morse makes a pile of money at the RV plant, he's foreman. I think it'd be hard to sink all that money into the C.P. but he does it every paycheck—when Lucy still lived here, she told me it always burned her up that he did that."

I stop. His *click* and *hum* machine keeps on. I think how Lucy Calhoun was ten years older than me and pretty, with straight hair, and didn't fool with me much. She sulked around with catalogs of clothes she couldn't have and never looked at *National Geographic*. She wanted out of here so bad, she grew a lump in her breast so Nancy would take her away. Lucy has two girls now. I guess they'll be there. At the burial.

"It's Christ's body," I say in a rush, to move faster than my sadness can. "We all make up the hands and feet of Christ Jesus, and all the parts. Each one has to be as important as the next, sharing all things in common. That's the C.P. In unison like a choir. That's how Leonard says it, even though not one of us can sing."

I pull at the sleeve of this black dress that doesn't fit right. They're supposed to be three-quarter sleeves, but my arms aren't like Lucy's, so the sleeves fall right at my elbow and wrinkle up and itch.

When I'm not speaking it's nice and silent in his room, it's a hush-room. Just his machine and the faraway sounds of people downstairs. People don't fill up Solomon's Porch, it's like they haunt it. They keep to themselves or they hang around it in tiny clumps like grass in the sidewalk cracks. But in my own room, I hear their noise like there's hundreds of people. That's because my room shares a wall with the full bath that everyone uses since the half bath downstairs is out of order. I hear all their bathroom sounds. I'm in the habit of listening close for them because I have to, so I don't walk in on somebody. We don't even lock the bathroom door, I suppose because of the angels. And whatever I hear, I picture. I hear Jude pee in the toilet. I hear it hit the water with a *pissss* and then I can picture his part. The part that bumps up the front of his pants just a little. I've seen it in drawings in Nancy Calhoun's home ec books, but I've never seen it out plain, on any man, not even in *National Geographic* because Carson tears out any naked pictures before she hands the magazines over to me. Sometimes I sit there picturing for longer than Jude's in the bathroom for.

But I hardly hear a thing when I sit here with Loomis's North. I'll just sit a spell by his bed. Maybe such a long spell that daylight will turn dark and I'll not have to go to the graveyard and lose my law-brother, my brother brother. My Wood full of secrets.

"Maybe I should tell you what I look like since your eyes are always shut." I rush on, running light with my tongue like never before, for he is so easy to talk to.

"I have curly brown hair, in clips right now."

I do not say that it's stringy and like a brier bush, ratty and halfway down my back, almost as long as Carson's.

"I have beautiful teeth and slender arms. And freckles." I scratch the insides of my elbows where the black sleeves crinkle.

"Sorry," I whisper because I'm lying.

I have no freckles, only a mole by my mouth. I have crooked teeth and I can't get braces because C.P. rules say no money for cosmetics. My arms are bigger and stronger than they should be for a twelve-year-old girl. Truth be told, I'm man-like and I even have a little moustache starting over my lip, like a shadow, but it will probably get dark and I'll probably grow hairs out of my chin like Nancy Calhoun. When we sit working on sewing tasks, I want so bad to reach over and pull out her chin hairs.

Not to mention that I'm sitting in stinky blood. Even after three days of it, I can't situate the Always pad right. Nancy has left both kinds under the sink, but I saw a Tampax and said, "No way," and chose the pad with wings that stick underneath. I thought I'd stop noticing it, but I don't. I notice it like a person hearing that tap leak into the sink all night. Drives me crazy.

"I have beautiful eyes," I say.

And that's the truth. They're Wood's. Maybe he can still see through my hazel eyes.

Then there he is, in a full picture I've blocked from my mind in this hush-room, pulling in all the other C.P. people instead, for Loomis's North to see, like paper dolls to keep our minds busy. Now, there is Wood laughing, of all things. Holding a tape recorder to his mouth to record, but he's laughing too hard to speak. My eyes are dry as drought. They ache back into my head, all the way down my throat to my chest. I jump up and go to the window that faces the Bueys. I know by now that jumping and rushing and barging in won't bother Loomis's North one bit.

"Vaughn Buey teases me when he looks at my eyes," I say. "He puts his hand on his cheek and says, 'Oh me, oh my,' joking with my name. I go by 'Omi'—Oh *me*, not Oh my. But it doesn't matter right now."

I decide to say it out loud, to this man who can hear me clear as day, says Jayne the sweet hospice nurse, all the way up to the end.

"Today they're going to bury my brother. Today I am Mara."

I am bitter. Not pleasant, not delight.

"You understand?" I ask, and I know he does. Loomis's North doesn't seem bothered by me.

I see the black shade go up in Vaughn's room. I can see into his window. He's awake and stands with his shirt off. I suppose he can see me like a shadow-shape through this thin curtain. I don't move. I don't look away.

This morning they found another jar of flowers on the back steps, left there with egg delivery by the Amish boy, Spencer Frye, but who for? It was more flowers than ever, snowballs and zinnias and daisies and blue ones turning to purple. All the red zinnias around the edge in a rim—he took care with that—so their strong stems could hold up the floppy ones. He has left a jar of flowers with the eggs every morning for the last three days.

The first day after it happened, Jude brought the jar to my law-mother Carson and said, "They must be for you, Sister Carson."

"How thoughtful," she said, all empty eyed. She stood back and touched one of the million bobby pins that held up the twisted braid of her long hair, but she did not touch those flowers. "They're for all of us in this time of loss," she said, like a scolding for Jude who'd singled her out. Like a program book about the C.P. All things in common, even our sadness, even our Time of Loss that, for me, will never run out.

Well, I touched them.

I stroked them each one on their stiff stalks then flimsy stalks and color-changing heads. They're for me, I thought to myself. Spencer Frye would leave them for me and for Wood and for nobody else.

"Don't ruin them now," said Carson to me. She took my Ball jar of flowers out of Jude's hands and into the Sanctuary, the big room at the front of the house facing Tyrone Road, the road through Dunlap that takes you from the hardware store to the traffic light and bars. I watched her feet as she walked without lifting them, just shuffling, like scooting toys across the floor. There was wind between my law-mother and me, blowing her that way and me the other way, so mad I could spit, out the backdoor to my mosaic wall.

I went down the back steps, past the loose brick that always pinned down Spencer Frye's dollar until he took it at 5 a.m. each day and gave the eggs and gave and gave, as long as the summer shot up flowers. He must pick them in the dark, just before daylight. Had he been standing there right then, in his white collared shirt, maybe I would have been able to cry. I would have run and got the radio from Wood's room and played it for Spencer who is not allowed radio by the Amish. They have rules like we do. "WAJR, a fine morning it is here in Elkhart County," the voice would say, and then the top hits, and in flashes of static when the signal gave out, we'd hear Wood's voice talking.

But Spencer Frye was not there.

I sleep late now, so I will never see him or even hear his horse and buggy.

I crossed to my mosaic wall through Jude's garden barrels. I sat on my stool, which is an overturned barrel too shallow to plant in. There was a gulf between the wall and me that felt like a year. But really I'd been working on it just the other day, before my blood appeared and Wood disappeared. I vowed right then, sitting on my stool with one finger touching a glued-on shard of plate, not to work on the wall ever again, even though it's really about done, if you minus the grouting work you do at the end. What for if he couldn't see it?

It's been my spring art project for the home school and was going to be a surprise for him. They used to think art would bring me out of my shell; that's why they let me paint the walls of my room four different colors. I wish they'd bring somebody in to do art like Nancy does home economics. Sue Calhoun's got no knack for art, just gives me the book to figure it out for myself, and I do pretty well. I chose the mosaic because of the types they showed in the book, full of color pieces like a million cat's eye marbles in some pattern. Besides that, there weren't too many other good projects to choose from—paper dolls and sock puppets. I chose collage for snowy days inside and mosaic for outside when the sun shone. And I knew right where I wanted to make it for him: on the cinder-block wall that Vaughn Buey's brother Odell built in back, to cover the crawl-space hole where rats were getting in. Odell has a real square head and looks like the cinder blocks they make where he works. He built it years ago, and right away, Leonard painted the blocks white and tried to show the Jesus Movie there for the boys in the apartments and other kids in Dunlap. He put up fliers at Kroger and Chalkers pool hall and the hardware, and showed the movie about Jesus's life and times every Friday till the projector broke. Nobody but Lucy and me came to see it, because we had to. And we never got a new projector, or a VCR either, so Leonard changed his tune. He said the Gospel needs nothing added, no modern pizazz. Funny how he explains things that way instead of saying we don't have the money.

So, no movies on that white wall, and it was perfect for my mosaic. I had no tiles or pottery like the book called for, but in the back it said I could make them from broken plates and vases. We don't waste dishes in Solomon's Porch, but Jude gave me some mismatched saucers on the sly. And Chastity Buey works at Cindy Lane's, the diner at the edge of town; she gave me their busted bowls and plates, deep brown ones and pearly blue ones with flecks of gold.

I was supposed to sketch it up first, to figure out my pattern. But for some reason I didn't want to. I wanted to dream the mosaic and let it grow chunk by chunk. I didn't flip through books for ideas like I do for collage. I started the first day the sun shone warm enough in March. I guess it was right after the spring farm trip that Wood came home for, it was right after he left again to finish his first year of Bible college learning radio broadcasting. I busted each plate in a pail with pliers. The first day, I cut up my hands, so I wore a pair of Jude's work gloves after that. Piece by piece on the wall. And it did come to me like in a dream, where to glue each chunk.

I guess since it came on its own, I didn't really come up with it. I just caught it, like in a butterfly net. It's not a butterfly, the pattern, but as I sat on the stool that morning, missing my jar of flowers and looking at the mosaic wall with that wide gulf between me and it—like the Gulf of Mexico except it was full of the Time of Loss instead of saltwater and sails—I saw that it was something with wings. Or it would be, if I finished it, which I'd just vowed never to do. In the curve of pieces, I could almost see a feather pattern.

"It's too bad," I said. I touched another shard, one of Chastity's blues.

Wood's secret rushed into my mind, but rushed in wearing its cloak so I could not know it. "Things with wings," he'd said, laughing.

Then a hand on my shoulder and I jumped.

"Easy, girl," said Vaughn Buey to me, coming out of nowhere.

I rubbed my arm like a bee had stung. Vaughn wore his flannel shirt open in front. He is skinny and tight and smooth in the chest since he's started at the RV plant. His eyes squinted in the sun, and his dark hair was smooshed on one side. He'd just gotten up. His eyes had hollows.

"Mom was making a racket in the kitchen. I couldn't sleep in." Vaughn stretched his arms up in a yawn. His loose jeans slipped lower than his bellybutton. He's seventeen. Too old to talk to me when Odell's around. But Odell's mostly at Chalkers pool hall, and when it's just me and Vaughn, it's different. Like last fall when they cut down the big hickory tree out front of Solomon's Porch. He sat in the grass and watched with me. I knew he was as sad as me to watch the old tree die. Mostly he teases.

"Omi," he said, "I'm real sorry about Wood."

I rubbed both arms, lots of bees stinging me. I said nothing. Vaughn looked at my mosaic like he'd looked at that hickory getting cut.

"They having a wake?" he asked.

"A wake?" My voice cracked because it did not want to come out. He is not awake, I thought, and a big part of me is not awake either.

"I mean a viewing. At the funeral home." Vaughn would not

tease me now. My tap leaked a drop into the Always pad and I crossed my legs standing up, like I had to pee.

"We don't believe in that," I said. "The body's just a vessel that the soul leaves behind when it goes up to God." I covered my mouth, my crooked teeth.

"Fuck," he said, in a wondering way and not a mean way. He's gotten that mouth from working at the plant. It's vile there, says Morse, mostly black men and the Spanish-speaking who only know dirty words in English.

Vaughn and I just stood there. I rubbed my arms, and he scratched his chest where his skin was tan from going shirtless. My arms were dark, too, from working out in the sun so many days. I would lose that now and go pale as a fish.

He spit on the ground by a barrel of Jude's tomato plants. He touched my mosaic on the same blue piece I'd touched before, the piece from his mom's plates. "What's it going to be?" he asked.

It was going to be wings. With feathers of every color.

"Nothing," I said. "I won't finish it."

I wanted right then to be finished with my life. To feel that kind of relief instead of the soda and vinegar making a volcano in me like a home-school science experiment. Then Vaughn touched my cheek. He didn't even ask. My volcano went from my brain to my fingers and right to the center of my eyes. Burning, but no tears. I pulled my face away. The *vroom* of Odell's motorcycle came down Tyrone Road, then up the alley. Vaughn backed away and went into his house. Their screen door had tape covering the tears.

I thought: if I could finish up now, with this life, that would be fine with me. I could see whether it's true about the body. Whether or not the soul leaves it alone and empty.

The next morning, the second day of my Time of Loss, here came Nancy Calhoun with a new sewing kit.

She had trouble finding me because nobody had seen me or heard me or felt me. I was in the room with Loomis's North learning his oxygen machine and learning the ways of the sweet and sour hospice nurses, Jayne and Regina. Both women wore the same style of pullover blouse and white pants, but Jayne's big blouse had teddy bears all over. She says funny things like, "We all need a little sugar for the sting." Her eyes are always wet; she's like a woman-form of Jude, except he's stick skinny and quotes Scripture and calls me "sister." Jayne doesn't call me "sister," or "Omi" even. She calls me "Ruthie," from my middle name. Her grandbaby's called Ruthie, she says, and I look a smidge like her. Regina, dressed in navy blue and wearing gloves, does the medicines through the IV, but it's Jayne in the teddy bears who handles his body. So gently he can't possibly hurt from it.

It's Jayne who tapes the cotton balls behind his ears under the curl of his oxygen tubing. It's Jayne who pinches a clip on each tube so to pull him free to bathe in the bathroom next to my closet-room. At his bath I figured she'd finally shoo me, the way I was haunting around, but she knew something about me. Come on in, she said. The first man I'd seen naked, and I looked shyly at the sink fixtures for most of it. But I sensed it wasn't wrong—my watching—because Jayne didn't shoo me and, more so, because that bath was like him getting baptized. She held one hand to his thin back and sponged with the other—the water warm but not too warm—his chest shoulders hair. Silent silver-white, in the name of the Father, Son, and Holy Ghost.

Afterward, I carried the bundle of towels and soaps for Jayne as she carried him to his bed, like a child. Regina started hooking him back up to things. Then I heard Nancy's voice in the hallway, and my law-father Leonard's, too.

The door opened a crack. I met Leonard's eye and felt caught. Regina ignored him like she ignores everything and did the blood pressure. Jayne looked at the door and said, "Ruthie, fold up those towels." I was Ruthie. I set the soaps down and folded carefully. But I watched the eye in the door. There could have been sadness wanting to come through, but it didn't know how.

The door shut again.

I heard Nancy. "She shouldn't be so near a dying person. Now of all times."

Leonard said something too quiet to hear. Whatever it was, it made Nancy mad and she raised her voice. "Have you even talked to her? Any of you? Don't pull that holier than thou. She's your daughter. Are you listening to me?"

I heard Leonard going down the stairs. Fine with me.

Nancy came into the room and Jayne beamed a welcome. I was enfolded in Nancy's bloomy sleeves. "It's okay," she cooed, and she took me by the hand, led me down to the Sanctuary where her sewing kit sat. And also a portable Singer sewing machine. And also the jars of flowers that I wasn't supposed to touch since I might ruin them.

Nancy muttered something about everyone drinking Kool-Aid for Leonard one of these days, a reincarnated Jim Jones.

"You believe in reincarnation?" I asked her. I'd read about it in *National Geographic*, the one on India that I kept under my bed.

"Oh, Omi," she cooed. She took my cheeks in her hands. I pulled away. Why was everyone touching my face without asking? *The Macedonian Call* had had a feature on reincarnation, too, on how it was a lie. I hadn't kept that issue under my bed; no pictures in it. Nancy's look wrapped me in that pity-cloth of pinpricks.

As usual, she pushed the sewing kit aside and started talking menstruation. I could tell she wanted to celebrate it—she had said that it was something girls should celebrate—but she felt too sorry for me. From her purse she pulled out a pocket calendar with two kittens on the cover, "1986" in pretty purple bubble letters under their paws. She opened it to June and gave me a pen.

"Right here on June 14. Draw yourself a little star, Naomi. That's right. Now count thirty days ahead on the calendar. One, two, three," she counted, up to July 14. "Now draw a little box for your next star. For when you menstruate next month, so you can be prepared." She looked sadder and sadder. "It might come earlier or later at first. It might take a while for your body to find its rhythm."

I guessed that my law-mother Carson had told her about my blood, because I'd never breathed a word. She must have found the pink wrappers in the bathroom trash bucket.

"It stinks," I said to Nancy. Maybe it was Carson who had told her about Wood, too. Or maybe it was in the paper. Or on the radio.

"What does, sweetheart?"

"The blood," I said.

"It's just your natural female odor," said Nancy Calhoun to me. "You're a flower opening up." She made a big bloom with her hands.

"I tried Carson's Secret deodorant under my arms. It's 'Spring Fresh' but it didn't cover it up. And it didn't smell like spring, or like summer either." "Summer Fresh," I thought to myself. That would smell more like dirt. Like sun and plowing and dirt and small sheds.

Nancy said I would need to wash every day now. Like dew on my flower, she said, spreading her hands again so her sleeves flopped. They flopped and it felt like my thoughts scattered out of them like moths: I thought about summer smelling of dirt, burying bodies that might or might not reincarnate—Wood, where will you be? In a cave in India with snakes that glow in the dark? Will I know you then?

I was folded up in those sleeves again, and she started crying. She had asked Leonard, mad, "Have you even talked to her," but she wasn't speaking either. Not to the Omi who was growing old in the Time of Loss.

"Come here now," Nancy said. She wiped her eyes, careful with her eye makeup that smeared anyway. "I've brought you a new project today. Want to see?" She tried to be all sunshine and eager.

It was a new pillow kit, still in its cellophane. She opened it and pulled out bright bright fabrics, three different blues and a cloud-white for the backing, spools of thread, a booklet of directions. "Oversized Envelope Pillow Slip," it said on the booklet, with a picture of how it would look when it was done.

"Jayne needs me to fold towels upstairs," I said. I had no interest in the blues, each one patterned wildly, in swirls, in fishes, in ripples. Like if you'd lay your head on that pillow, you would hear the ocean.

"Now, honey."

"I have to go. I'll take this and study it later. I have work to do." And I gathered up the spilled-out pillow kit. I put it back in its bag in an ugly way, I knew, the fabric all crumpled up.

"Sweetheart," Nancy said, crying again through her fake sunshine. But I took the kit and ran out of the Sanctuary, up the stairs. Right into my closet-room with the four walls all sounding out their own loud colors. Nancy didn't follow. I shoved the sewing kit under my bed where I keep my favorite magazines. Where I keep all my collages, too, the one on top of the pile my most recent, all its pictures from the *National Geographic* special issue on India. I pulled it out and wiped away a ball of dust and hair. My last collage. Like mosaic, I decided never to do another. What for if he can't see it?

But I've been thinking.

Today the nurses came and went quickly. They didn't ask about my black dress. I spent all of yesterday with them and with Loomis's North, and nobody bothered me. Not Nancy Calhoun, not Carson or Leonard. Only Jude one time, without a word, to give me some crackers with jam, which I ate like I was starving.

I've been thinking about showing my last collage to Loomis's North.

Once the nurses left this morning, I went and got the collage from under my bed. I gave the pillow kit an extra shove. I came back into the hush-room, the white white room, and put the collage under my chair.

Now I stand in the quiet like the quiet is a grove of trees. I'm done talking about myself and about this uncommon place called the C.P. I see out the window, into Vaughn's window where he stands with no shirt. Like a stare down until we laugh, but we don't laugh. I expect him to look away first, and I wish he would because if he sees clear through this curtain he can see that my dress doesn't fit right, just a tight sack for my body. I think he's going to turn away, but it's me. I go back to my chair and pick up my collage.

"See?" I say, then I remember I'm through with talking. So I just point and scoot closer to Loomis's North, careful with his breath machine. We're close enough to touch, except for the bed rail.

I call this one "Indigo Dancing to Red." It's all women dressed in saris. In India they wear them, like scarves stretched into sheer dresses of every color. For Loomis's North who has his eyes shut but who might be able to see up till the end, like he can hear, I point out the way the dance goes, like a story, from corner to corner to corner of the paper.

Here in this photo the women dry their clean saris on the beach, flap and flap, a mile of sari-waves between the pairs of women. And smaller, in the background, more women drying more saris, just silhouettes. And once they're dry, the drums start softly. The next picture glued: one woman is resting from the laundry work, her belly showing, turquoise sari around her hips and down her legs, turquoise and silver up top, her arms stretched back. She's ready to spring—and to the next one— she walks down marble steps, glancing back at me, her back bare now, and the sari is peach skin on her brown skin, draping down over her arms, a sash, a movement. She bows in the next one, her hair pinned up but not like Carson's in a tight braid-twist: it's in a loose black swirl with white flowers stuck in. She reaches to swish the sari or touch her toe or something else, with the drumming louder and a tinkling of bells, till the next one: a woman old like Loomis but in a yellow sari with embroidered green draped over her head like in a Bible picture—how I think Naomi looks in the Book of Ruth—and a great gold ring through her nose. Her hands up, ready to clap for the dancers. And next: a photo looking from the sky, looking down on girls and women, each in their own flowing color, indigo to red, dancing on a floor of tiles of four-legged stars, this way, that way. I move the collage in the air to show him. If only he could see, if only he could hear their million bracelets jangling and the loud drumming.

And then it's the last one.

Slow slow, and hush.

The last picture glued is after the dance is done and the women go home, all except one. That one stands in the stone archway. Her sari is the deepest pink-zinnia color, trimmed in gold. It touches the stone floor. She stands clasping her arm, outside a big dark door that is padlocked. She cannot get in. Her dance is over.

See? I have cut carefully. From a photograph of me, I've cut out my face and pasted it here, where her lovely face was. I've drawn a tiny diamond in my nose like she had. So it is me in the zinnia-gold sari after the dance.

"See?" I say out loud, forgetting to be quiet.

Always I make these collages to show Wood. With some kind of theme, like women in saris, men in hats, or kids playing in water. Or all things red. All things wild. It comes from a game he played with me. He would say "things that are free," and we'd go back and forth: love, Jude's garden goods, dirty water from Elkhart River, salvation, tree bark. Then he'd wrap them all together and make a story, like the dance of the saris.

I hold the dance still. Wood's secret comes back to me: on the tractor on the spring farm trip, he stood up like you're not supposed to when it's moving. Things with wings, he said. He laughed, and I was afraid he'd fall, but I got busy in my mind with a flood of things with wings, endless things.

"I want to tell you something, Omi," he said.

Bats, planes, dragonflies, I thought.

"Omi—" but the tractor lunged and Wood had to sit and steady it.

Monarchs, I thought, and starlings and golden eagles.

Mr. Booth hollered, ran over and gave us a talking-to. "One time a boy got run over by a plow," he yelled. "How would you like to be cut up like that?"

"Angels," I said.

The farmer didn't hear. Wood sank his eyes in mine, my eyes in his. We weren't alone ever again that day, just the two of us. When we got home, he went back to Bible college, to finish his first year. And I never heard his voice again.

I hear a knock at the door.

"Sister Omi."

It's Jude. It's time.

"Sister Omi."

I fold my collage, indigo to red. I slip it under his pillow, and Jude comes for me.

MY RADIO RADIO

SOMEBODY HAS robbed all the flowers from their Ball jars and stuck them into one old fishbowl that's not as pretty. I carry the bowl of flowers before Carson can say no. I can hardly see. Just red and blue and green leaves, a jungle of flowers that I follow into the rented van and ride. Jude cries the whole way to the graveyard, my flowers muffling his sound. I whisper to Jude beside me, "Is Loomis's North coming too? In another van?"

Whimper, whimper, says Jude.

"I would like it if he was there," I say.

"Sister Loomis can't even come," he manages to say. "We have to walk up the steep side. It's too hard for her." So that's where he'll be buried. That steep straggly side of the cemetery, the side that butts up against the chain-link fence, by the Wendy's parking lot.

And it *is* steep, tricky for me while I'm carrying the flowers.

When we get up there, I finally set them down, heavy as a bowling ball at my feet. We circle up then. It is Morse and Sue, Nancy and Lucy and her two girls hopping up and down till Lucy says, "Stop," Vaughn and Odell, Chastity who steps aside for a cigarette because she can't help it, Jude and Carson and

Leonard. And me. We all hold hands and I shrink for the feel of Leonard's skin. Lucy looks like a fashion model and stands shyly by Sue, her law-mother who watches Lucy's girls like she's hungry, for she hardly sees them. Chastity smokes it fast and tosses it, comes back to the circle. She wears a black shawl over her striped waitress outfit. She must have work right after. Say good-bye to Wood and go ask, "How you want your steak?" and "What dressing and how many Cokes?" I wish I could go bring people Coke after Coke and never stop. Vaughn puts his arm around her because she is shaking. I look at Carson and then back at Chastity, and it's hard to say who is Wood's mother. Law-mother, mother mother.

Vaughn is in a dark blue suit. That surprises me, like I expected he would come with no shirt, just chest skin breathing up, breathing down. Vaughn who's had lots of girls and who touched my cheek with a hand smelling of motor oil. He looks my way.

And I know how I look. Too big, too bushy headed with hopeless hairclips, too childlike with this cream-scalloped collar. Too grown-up with womb's blood coming, and too used up in a black pleated dress that falls to my shoes, which should be new but aren't. They're shaped to Lucy Calhoun's foot, haunted by Lucy Calhoun's foot. I slip them off, as if to give them back to her, and stay barefoot behind the cover of the fishbowl of flowers on the ground.

Two other C.P. people are buried here, men I never knew. They're the two Mennonite men who started the C.P. with Leonard way back. I examine one tiny headstone then the other, each with only a name. Phillip C. Cogdale. A. C. Howard. Such pitiful, ugly little grave markers. I look around for something bigger and made of marble. Then I let my eyes land on Wood.

He is there in a not-so-fancy coffin beside a mound of dirt beside a black hole in the ground. I don't know how he got there, up on cement blocks like Vaughn's car when the engine's broke down. Or how long he's been lying there with the lid open to the wind and the sun and the night and the birds. I did not expect the lid to be up. Maybe the soul hasn't yet flown and they're giving it a last chance to decide: stay with the body or fly. I can't tell what the soul decides. I just look and look. I see and see and see, memorizing my brother deep in my deep-freezer mind. But I'm too far away from him so I break from the circle and go close. There's the edge of the unfancy casket like there's the metal bed rail by Loomis's North.

I stay in my hermit-crab shell and don't wail, don't even cry. I think that Lucy is looking at me wearing her dress and thinking I'm unnatural, weird, and stingy like everybody else in the Dunlap Fellowship of All Things in Common, with no natural tie to my law-brother. Let her think it. Let her feel sorry that she left me alone.

I hear her girls hop hopping again. "Stop," whispers Lucy, but they can't help it, their bodies are too small to contain them. I turn to see them playing with my jungle of flowers, plucking one each for their hair. I fly fast and rip the zinnia from the older girl's hair and clinch it. I crush it. The girl starts crying. Jude, too, louder than before. Sue Calhoun steps close to me and her law-grandbaby like she's going to scold me and have me apologize, but she just stands there and starts a sad hymn. Everyone joins but me, "Old Rugged Cross," and it sounds lousy because nobody can sing.

The red of the squeezed zinnia is painting my hand.

I don't need to look at Wood again. My photographic memory holds him right in the center of my brain, right beside my memory of the last time I saw him. Because—I am stunned—he wears no suit in the coffin. He wears the chore clothes that he wore last time we were together, on the spring farm trip. Brown corduroy pants. Each year they got shorter and shorter, but he's so slim, they still fit at the waist. He is a shabby chore boy going into the ground, not my Wood full of voices, not my radio radio, secret and secret, best brother of mine.

Leonard starts in with his sermon-voice, hands now clasped in front. I don't hear what he says sermon-wise, his real words, just the sound. I curl my toes into the grass and grip my zinnia and listen for his double-layer cake of kindness and scorn. But, no, it's a triple-layer cake, a quadruple-layer, so many layers that I quit the picture of the cake. His voice is layered like sedimentary rock.

One layer asks, Why waste a good suit on a body with no soul? Sell it, give it away to the orphan, the stranger, the needy with no face that Omi can recognize, and dress this body in old corduroy.

We cannot be selfish in our Time of Loss. That's another layer.

What does the suffering teach us? The next layer. The lesson that is written out for the common good all over Wood's body. God writes it in code on this body that may or may not still have a soul in it.

These are not Leonard's words. I don't care to hear his words. I just dig deeper and deeper like an archæologist working for *National Geographic*. And the deepest layer in the rock, a million years old, with dinosaur bone stuck in tar pit: that layer is sadness. That layer says, My boy my boy my boy.

Then it's Morse and Vaughn and Odell closing the lid, lifting the plain ugly coffin, lowering him down on ropes. It's not easy because of the steep slope. Wood rocks, Wood rustles. It's his legs rubbing together under the lid, the *ruff ruff* of his corduroy pants. Terror strikes me. His soul cannot choose—stay or fly? It's panicking.

I am ready for screams—I think of night terrors, the screaming fits Lucy told me she had, and Sue would not come to her till after they were all screamed out and Lucy was a sweaty mess in bed. Then the night terrors grew quiet and grew a lump in Lucy's breast. She had it for over a year and didn't tell because we had so little money, though Morse could have paid a doctor if he didn't sink it all into the Common Purse. She kept quiet till she finally told Nancy and Nancy took her away to emergency.

My mouth opens but no sound. Real terror is not a loud scream. Just quiet. The quiet terrors are the worst. It's the *ruff ruff* of his corduroy pants.

They're in a circle holding hands and singing hymns, but I don't join. My hand is a vice. I bleed my zinnia. I fly back toward the narrow pit for me and Wood alone. And *ruff ruff* I hear from his knees knocking. I sink and the pit becomes my deep-freezer mind stuffed full: there is Wood on the tractor, in his too-short corduroys and a T-shirt soaked with sweat from an eager spring sun.

I see him as he was three months ago, March. I stay in that picture and shut the rest out.

He came back from Indianapolis to visit, back from Bible college to do the annual farm trip with me. I hugged him so hard when he came in from Tyrone Road looking like a full-grown man at nineteen. Every year we went to the Booths' Mennonite farm where Leonard had been raised, so we would know our law-father's roots and the roots of the C.P. We always helped clear the fencerow and hack the rhubarb and plant the onion sets alongside Mennonite men in plain clothes and women in white caps. We always went to the dairy barn where they didn't use machines to milk, only strong hands. This time we started at the dairy because we wanted to keep cool, but it turned out hotter inside, from the hot hides of the cows. It was Spencer Frye doing the milking, hired on from the Amish farm farther out the straight county road. The Mennonites were plain but the Amish were plainer, we found out. "Hello," we three said. Wood and I brought Spencer pail after pail. Spencer watched me. I was wearing an old pair of Lucy's blue jeans and a knit top that rode up to show my belly if I wasn't careful, which I was. Sweat spread down the back of his white collared shirt.

"Here," said Spencer to me. "Your turn."

"Me?"

"Yes, you," Wood said. "Miss Omi Milkmaid." He laughed. He was not the backward boy I knew. He laughed at me and at his own happiness. Then I knew: that's what had made him look full-grown. A secret happiness had nudged my brother just beyond my reach. What was it? I wanted him to tell me.

I was terrible at milking. Just a tiny squirt from the teat. It hit the pail with a tin sound.

"You must grab with your whole hand," said Spencer in his odd, formal voice. He leaned close to me on the stool, his dark hair brushing my own. He wrapped a teat with his strong hand and yanked hard so a steady stream shot out. "See?"

I felt a stirring inside. I had stuck my hand in Vaughn's ball glove one time, and that was how the udder felt. Like leather that's had a hand stuck in it on lots of ballgame nights.

"Does she like it?" I blurted.

Spencer turned bright red. Wood howled and laughed. He

had brought his radio, the small one that tunes in and that also records to a tape, the radio he talked into in funny voices, whenever he was too shy to talk to the world. He put it to his mouth to record like this was some live radio show, but he was laughing too hard to speak.

"What's so funny?" I asked, mad.

Wood said it was nothing and tried to quit, but busted up again. "Nothing at all," laughing loud and leaving me out.

Spencer Frye was red as a beet and kept his eyes on Wood's radio.

I glared into the white patch of coarse hair on the cow's side and folded my arms across my chest where I was soft, where I was tender.

"You ever work a radio?" Wood said to Spencer, light and free as a lark.

Spencer shook his head. "No. It's not allowed in the Old Order."

"Well. Today you've got a radio." Wood tuned it in, fuzzy at first, turning the dial through static. A song caught. He turned it up loud and filled the hot barn with the pop song. I couldn't stay mad for too long.

When the teats were dry and the pails full, Spencer said we had to take the last two pails to the shed for cheese. The women in white caps had buzzed in and buzzed out all morning, taking the other pails away and frowning at the music.

"You two go ahead," Wood said and put his radio in his back pocket. "I'll go get the tractor key from Mr. B."

The wire handle cut into my fingers. Spencer and I set the pails on a concrete slab inside a tiny unpainted shed. An old refrigerator powered by extension cord sat in the corner, its racks taken out.

"They will skim off the cream for making cheese curd," said Spencer Frye.

I nodded, tugged down the bottom of my knit top. I asked if he did more than the milking.

"I do chickens, too. And sell the eggs." He stood close to me and looked at the walls that felt to me like they were moving in on us.

"This is the old laundry," he said. "See the big kettle on the woodstove? They used to heat the water there. We still use one like it at home." He sounded sorry. "Naomi, I am sixteen this month. Almost on *rumspringa*."

"On what?"

"Rumspringa. It is in our language. It means we turn sixteen and we are free to taste the world outside. Like radios." He pointed back toward the barn and smiled. "Like cars and anything else we want a taste of." He ran his fingers through his hair and I smelled the earthiness of his underarm. He looked at me like he knew something about me.

"At the end of rumspringa," he said, "we choose. Do I join church? Or do I join the world?" His eyes were ice-hot blue and did not let me move left or move right. He was not that different from us C.P. people who held back a little from the world and held things in common like Jesus said to. We used to be twenty families, but most people left—so they could buy things, Leonard always said, like Lucy Calhoun who wanted every dress in the Sears catalog. But maybe they wanted something else too. I wasn't sure I knew what the world tasted like.

"Omi!" Wood hollered outside. I heard the tractor idling. I held my breath and was not sure whether I wanted my brother to find me.

"Omi Ruth!"

My body was too small to contain me—the me that wanted the shed walls to push me up against Spencer Frye, and the me that wanted to call out to Wood whose happiness had grown him up and had shifted him, without warning, just beyond my reach.

"This is my only day with my brother before he leaves again," I whispered, more to myself than to Spencer. I ran outside then and Wood waved to me. I climbed onto the white tire guard, and we took off toward the plowed field ready to be disked by the line of sharp plates the tractor dragged behind it. I did not look back to see whether Spencer waved good-bye. I looked at the sky and at the plain dresses and pants swirling in the wind on the laundry line by the house, and at Wood driving the tractor with ease, his hair smooshed back and his jaw strong.

"Wait! Where are you going?" I yelled over the tractor rumble. Wood had steered us away from the field toward the gate that opened to the county road.

"This is our quick getaway!" he yelled back.

"What?"

"Hoooo!" he yelled and drove us on through the rough grass, this way, that way, toward the road then away from it, in a curve and zigzag that must have been the pattern of his happiness. I laughed and drank in his face. No, I ate it. I ate the light in his face and got so full, like after eating a seven-course meal. So full, but empty, too, because I could not eat it all. There was too much for me.

"How about a game?" he hollered.

"Yes!" I said. "You start." A game like we'd always played that would make us like we'd always been, knowing each other completely.

He stood up then, all the way up on the seat, as the tractor kept on.

"Wood, no!" I screamed.

He stuck his arms out, wobbling like a tightrope walker. He called out, "Things with wings."

I quit worrying that he'd fall and thought up my million things. Then he said softly, but I could somehow still hear him over the engine roar: "I want to tell you something, Omi—" Then the lunge of the tractor and he dropped into the seat. Here came Mr. Booth running like wild, yelling at us because, once, a boy had been killed that way. Wood cut the engine.

"Angels," I said with the engine still ringing in my ears.

Wood swallowed his secret and left.

Navy blue sleeves around me, and I think it's Vaughn, his suit. But, no, I'm surprised, it's Carson. One arm is stiff, one soft and dangly like it's broken. She doesn't hold me, she pulls me to get up. My knees in black pleats are in the dirt though the mound is gone. They have shoveled it. They have buried my brother Wood.

I wonder, what did his soul choose? After it panicked? My thoughts come in choppy water, like a lake before a storm. Once on a tractor, hold still and call out. I could not contain him, all his beauty, his big beating heart. Call on me. I will hear you. I'm big enough for your happiness now, big to contain you. Your soul with mine, there's room for both of us in here.

"I'm big enough now," I say out loud, my voice like sandpaper in my throat.

"You are," says Carson to me, brushing my hair from my face. "You're big enough, pull yourself up. Come on now."

I rise but do not wipe the dirt from Lucy's black dress. Morse and Sue are the first to go. Then I realize it's over. Climbing the steep hill before, I expected that leaving here would be impossible, but now it feels so easy. I'm almost eager to go. I thought I would want to stay long into the dark.

Why do you want to go? I ask myself. Why do you want to fly?

So I can get out of this terrible dress. So I can breathe. So I can sit in the hush-light by Loomis's North. So I can come back here alone. All of my reasons are true at once.

I look for the headstone to memorize it so I know where to come back to.

There, next to my fishbowl of flowers that someone has moved. A flat stone, with just his name.

Woodrun Leonard Wincott Jr.

It is plain and ugly and small like the two others. It is like a scrap of paper. Trashy.

"No," I say, looking at my law-father. His sedimentary-rock voice has a face as hard and as layered to match.

"What is it, Naomi?" He can sense my anger.

This is all there is above ground to say, Here I am. Me, Wood. Here I lie beside this chain-link fence in Dunlap, Indiana. There should be mosaic and radio and wings and a best poem from Jude's books and marble and blue glass. The gray stone should at least be blue. I look down to the rest of the cemetery like into a valley of beautiful old bones, tall white ones, marble ones, marking graves with chiseled messages of vanity. For I know Leonard thinks it vain.

"It should at least be blue," I say. I drop my dead, sad zinnia onto the tiny stone and follow the Calhouns down the steep path to the van.

I am even-keeled in my thoughts the whole drive back to Solomon's Porch, no more choppy water. It's a case of Clear Morning Mind, though it's afternoon. I understand that the old corduroy pants and the ugly stone marker are signs that Wood needs my help. It's like his soul has flown into me after all and is giving me instructions.

We come down Tyrone Road, pull into the alley. I race out of the van, up the back steps emptied of flower-jars, and burst into the kitchen. I find Loomis sitting there drinking coffee, her housecoat buttoned wrong. She clears her throat. She is sitting at the table set for a big meal. I blow past her into Wood's room, next to Loomis's room, next to Jude's. The door is shut but not locked, and I am right. There are cardboard boxes already half-full of Wood's things. His clothes and tapes, an old kite, his blanket and sheets.

"No, no, no," I say. I try not to smell him deeply because I have no time.

These things all gathered up to be given away and sold. Money, some to the Common Purse and some to places in *The Macedonian Call* where missionaries search for lost people to save. I want to save no one but Wood. I want to save this, his pair of red shorts, and this, his denim jacket, this, his undershirt. I hear them all coming in, coming after me, so I grab this, his radio that tunes in and records, and there's a box of his tapes. I have time to grab only one and run out his door.

"Sister Omi," Jude cries out.

Up the stairs in a flash, arms full of stolen things. And, like I've done before, I rush through the door into the corner room where Loomis's North lies still and silent with the *click whirr* like feathers falling.

"It's me. Naomi Ruth." I hold my breath. Let it go in a gust. No terrors here, shrill or quiet. I open the thin closet by the foot of his bed, hung with old coats and stuffed with boxes of I-don't-know-what. I scoot the boxes to make a cubby, and there I hide Wood's clothes and radio and tape. I quickly shut the door and then I'm full of my own rushing. It knocks me like a hard blow into the chair.

"It's me," I say again.

I was here just this morning. How can that be? I was so small then, and young, despite having become a woman. But I check, and there is my collage folded under his pillow. The nurses maybe saw it, maybe not. Time moves too fast. I think it bounces off me. I don't soak it into my skin, but he does, Loomis's North. That is why he glows up through the white, because he holds so much time inside. I don't hold much time inside, but, for now, I do think I have Wood's soul in me.

This is the Time of Loss. It's slow and I sit and soak. I stay.

I need this time to figure some things out—like how in the world I'm going to get a big beautiful marker for my brother Wood's grave.

DIVING FOR ABALONE

I COME down the stairs close to noon with an armful of white linens, and two black-pearl eyes look up at me.

I've been all morning at the chores Jayne has assigned. She makes up a list for each day of the week and puts "Ruthie" at the top and says I'm good help. Carson and Leonard probably frown on it, but they've never been good at talking to me and they're worse at it now, so they steer clear, and so do Sue and Nancy, maybe since home school is out for the summer. Only Jude tries to talk to me and tries to get me to walk to the end of the block to the hardware, but I always stop at the front door. I climb the stairs and run my hand along the paneling and step one foot then another on the floorboards, carefully, till I reach my room with its walls of four pretty colors, or the room that is still and white, the room of Loomis's North. Regina, sour as always, says I'm nothing special. She doesn't like that I sleep so late and come and start my chores in my nightgown, but Jayne says it's fine—it's the task that matters not the dress.

I didn't wear my nightgown this morning though because it's July 14, the Day of My Little Star, and here came my blood like

46

a train on time. I was solemn, I put on fresh underwear, plenty ready this time with a new package of Always pads. I put on jean cutoffs and a snug blouse of Lucy's and got to work switching out the colostomy for Loomis's North.

"It's just me," I said to him, making sure he felt no shame since I felt none. I'd expected to feel ashamed, the first time I put my hands on him. I'd expected all kinds of things: that he'd feel like a big doll since he never got up and walked, that he'd break easily, or make some sound or wake up and ask me my name even though I'd told him already. And I'd expected Vaughn to tease me and Odell to say dirty things about me touching a man's body, but they are far from me now in their house next door. I just see Vaughn pass his window sometimes and hear Odell's motorcycle, like they're a whole country away. And I felt no shame because I knew Loomis's North needed me, and he was no doll: though his bones were delicate, he was real and strong enough. The chest beneath his white undershirts always moved up and down like any sleeping person's. He was calm and it calmed me to lotion his hands and salve his feet and put new cotton balls where the oxygen tube hooks his ears, to keep his lips wet enough with the little sponge in the glass. Here was someone like nobody else in the world, someone who could keep my secrets—like the many designs I dream up and describe for Wood's grave marker—someone who could almost keep me from being afraid.

This morning, like always, Jayne rolled him softly left and I undid the sheet and put a clean one; she rolled him right and I tucked the other side. Then I swathed him up good with two clean top sheets because his skin can get cool. Like swaddling a baby, Jayne says. Touching him makes me feel steady, but also something else that I cannot say, for I do not know it. I touch him no more roughly than snow. This man like a bed of moss receiving my snow.

I felt pride this morning, for my blood came right on day thirty, even though Nancy said it would take me a while to find my rhythm. I was prepared and careful. Then I was doing my nurse-work for Loomis's North and the chores kept me upstairs all morning till I was half-starved. I gathered up the sheets to wash and headed for the laundry room off the kitchen.

So I was feeling my strength, feeling grown, when I trailed down the steps on my way to the washer and found this girl sitting at the kitchen table like she's waiting for lemonade.

First thing I notice: her black eyes.

Second thing: her bushy yellow hair, curly as mine but pretty.

"It wasn't locked, so I came on in," says the girl to me.

Third thing I notice is a curve of sadness in her shoulders, like a weight is there I can't see, a weight inside and not out. But she smiles wide and says, "I like that pretty star window you can see from the road."

I don't speak, just sit down at the table across from her. My arms still bunch the sheets into my chest. She goes tall as she stands, in a pink long-sleeved sweater that falls to the knee, green leggings underneath that disappear into big black boots. She's older than me, but not by much. Her hair is so huge and wild, in long spirals like water spraying perfectly from her head. It occurs to me she might help me with my horrible hair.

The girl reaches down into a dirty duffle bag. I see the dark roots of her hair where the bleach hasn't touched. "I brought in your mail," she says. "If there's one thing I can tell you, it's to bring folks their mail. You give them mail and they think surely they know you. I did it once in Detroit when I smelled chicken from the street window, you can get drunk on fried-chicken smell. I carried in this woman's mail and took a quick peek at the picture frames on her mantle, I convinced her I'd gone to kindergarten with her daughter in the photos. I never seen the girl before, but the lady bought it and served me up a heaping plateful." She smoothes the front of her sweater and hands me the bundle of mail so that I have to let loose of the white sheets. On top is a new *National Geographic* and on the cover, a naked woman diving from a rowboat.

"The others all came down already," the girl says, "but I saved the mail for you. I was waiting for you." There's that sad curve to her back, but she's trying to act like it's not there.

I look at the naked woman on the cover, then at this girl who seems to know me but is a stranger to me. Her voice has a funny drawl, like one of Wood's radio voices, it's lazy. Her sturdy boots clomp on the floor as she sits back down. She looks like she walked here in those boots, all the way from Detroit. Maybe she did.

"They're all in that room there." She nods toward the Sanctuary. "Thinking on whether I can stay or not. Looks to me like you got space." Her eyes sweep the big kitchen where the pots hang and the hood shadows the green stove top and the plates and plates in the open cupboard wait for some big crowd for dinner. I stare into the cover of the *National Geographic* with all its pages still intact, a naked woman diving headfirst. This girl got it from the mailbox before Carson could tear off the cover. It's the first naked picture I've seen, except for Nancy Calhoun's diagrams that have no hair or shadow or softness or sag. No diving pose.

She says, "You don't say much. That's fine. Bet you got good reason, mmhmm?" She says *mmhmm* at the end like seeing whether I'm awake.

"Can you get my hair to look like yours?" I surprise her with my voice. I surprise me and cover my crooked teeth with my hand.

She cocks her head and a silver hoop earring glints from somewhere underneath her hair, like tinsel in a tree. "You just need some pomade," she says. "It'll piece out," and she tugs down one of her own coils that springs back like a wonder. "I'm Tracie."

"Omi Ruth," I say.

"Nice to know you, Miss Omi."

Then the door to the Sanctuary opens and first to come out is Jude, still in his breakfast apron. Tracie stands again, nervous, and the wide neck of her sweater slips almost off her shoulder. I see her deep tan skin, lovely bones underneath it in fine ridges, and I see Jude's eyes trail along there. Tracie straightens the sweater like readying for a photo.

Out comes Loomis with a dinner roll in her hand. Then Leonard, Carson, and Sue in a row. That's our big crowd. Morse is at the plant. Something about Tracie's sturdy boots makes me notice how Sue and Carson wear dresses they could float away in, and it's like they cling to Leonard with his tree-stump legs so to be sure they don't. Like they're afraid, and I'm trying to tell whether I'm just like them.

It's Leonard who will speak and I know he's not willing to let her stay. He's in his ugly tan pants, combing at his neat moustache, and I'm trembling inside like a bell struck. I realize how badly I want this girl to stay, to help me with my hair, to teach me to walk around in big boots. For, though I'm feeling grown and proud these days, after they buried my Wood I've stopped going outside the house, like the world is all rushing water and I stay at the water's edge. There's a part of me that wants to jump in but it's true I'm like Carson in her careful coiled-up braid, and like Sue who's part ghost. I'm too afraid of floating away and drowning.

Leonard begins in his layer-cake voice, extra layer of icing to make him sound regretful. "Miss Casteel, we've discussed your situation, asking guidance of the Lord. As we mentioned this morning, this is a household of all things in common. We share our food and our modest incomes." He goes on to list the founding principles that he often recounts like somebody's interviewing him for a history. Simplicity, discipline, brotherhood. The city on a hill he and the two Mennonite men dreamed up for this old hotel plus two houses, and now it's dwindled down to the seven of us. "When we have faced scarcity," he says, "the good Lord has seen us through. That said, we've recently seen—"

"I'm sixteen years old. I can drive a car and I do good housework." Tracie puts one fist on her hip and Leonard jolts, not used to being interrupted.

"You got cooking to do," she goes on, "I can whip it up and I can do the wash, too. I come out of Detroit. Lived there with my mama who worked for Ford double shift, so I can take care of myself. Mama and Daddy are both dead now and I get a good-size check from the government and I can dump it in your pocket first of every month."

They stare. Carson looks at me and I hide the *National Geographic* in my armful of sheets. I get a picture in my mind of the city of Detroit, a real city on a hill, and a Ford factory bigger than Dunlap's RV plant, and noisier, a picture too big for Solomon's Porch where we all stand staring at Tracie Casteel. And then I picture a *mama* and *daddy*, words I never use for Carson and Leonard, and both her parents are dead—is that the curve of sadness? I clutch the sheets and edge toward her.

"She can sleep in my room," I say, "so you can still rent the others. There's that bed frame nobody's using, in the room with Loomis's North."

"That's kind, Sister Omi," says Jude.

Leonard folds his arms and replants his feet on the floor, reminding everybody who's in charge. "Now, you didn't let me finish, Miss Casteel." It's her name he says, but he's looking at me. "Though we have little in earthly goods in this house, the stranger is always welcome. Hospitality to all, the lowly and the high. You're welcome to stay with us. And if you want to give of your resources, well, you may do it freely, under no compulsion." It's a new, thicker icing now, after hearing about that government check.

Tracie gives a nod, a little curtsy that looks funny to me, like she's teasing. She says "thank you" and reaches for her duffle then stops. "Just one more thing though. I'm pregnant, about four months along. But I ain't been sick since the first month, so I shouldn't give you no trouble."

They stare again. Sue and Carson look at Tracie's middle. She stretches her pink sweater taut, says, "You can see a little rise there if you look close." She meets my eyes. "I'm mighty glad to hear your all's verdict. I'll just take my things up."

Tracie hefts her duffle bag onto her shoulder before their gaze can leave her belly. "Come on, Omi Ruth," she says. "You can show me around."

A flapping in my chest shocks and thrills me. I don't miss a beat; I carry the dirty linens with the photo of the naked diver nestled deep in the bundle. I follow the green leggings and black boots up the staircase, like this girl is leading me to my own room and it's me who's seeing it for the first time.

"You painted this room yourself, I bet," says Tracie to me.

She settles onto my blue and white gingham bedspread that's gone threadbare in spots. "The walls are like a circus tent. We're the center of the Big Top, Miss Omi."

It's true, though I've never seen it that way before. My room's a tiny, old walk-in closet they put a window in; my window faces the one across the alley, in the apartments next door, a big-box air conditioner that never runs. Blue, green, violet, yellow. Each wall they had let me paint a different color, thinking it would help bring me out of my shyness, but it didn't. Like a circus tent indeed. There's a flower-decorated chest of drawers that we'll move over to make room for her bed. Everything's looking new, but shabby too. The paint is peeling around the window.

"It's peeling a little," I say.

She comes over to me in the doorway and takes the sheets I'm still clasping, magazine hidden inside. She dumps them on my bed by her duffle. "Just gives the place personality. Circus is rough, girl. Elephants and trapeze artists—all that stomping and twirling's gonna give some wear."

"You're strange," I say. I smile, I can't help it, I cover my mouth. She's rubbing her belly and looks tired. "And you have an accent," I say.

"Do I? It's how folks talk where I come from."

"From Detroit?"

"Look who's a chatty-box all of a sudden. That's good." Tracie wipes sweat from her temples and neck. It strikes me that she's wearing a heavy sweater in the heat of July. She unsnaps a front pocket of her bag. "I lived in Detroit most my life, but I come from Coal Lick. Little mountain town in West Virginia." She pulls out a postcard, creased and soft. "That's it there. Where it's dark before it's dark cause the valley walls are so steep they block the sun."

I hold the postcard with care. A tiny ring of houses in the middle of mountains bushy with fall trees, all gold and red. Houses swallowed up.

"I guess I still have a coal-town voice," she says. "I left there with Mama as a little girl, but we headed to Detroit with the others, after the mines put everybody out. So we set up our own little Coal Lick near the train tracks and the river. Mama thought it'd be good to get me out of coal dust, but Detroit's covered in black. It runs on that coal."

I hold out the postcard to give it back.

"You can keep that," she says. The ring of houses. The dark before it's dark.

I want to give Tracie Casteel something of my own, because she's tired and she's strange. I look around my room. I think about my collages and favorite magazines, but I'm not sure she won't laugh at them, child's play.

"I have lots of Always pads you can use," I say. "I'm real prepared." Then she's laughing a little.

"Awful sweet, Miss Omi, but I won't be needing those." She pats her stomach. "You don't bleed when you're pregnant, don't you know?"

"Oh." My face goes hot. Nancy Calhoun has told me that—of course she has—but only with charts and plastic wombs and books, not a real live woman with pretty hair and a small lump in her middle. Then I think: a baby means sex, and I know that from books, too. Who is the law-father, I wonder, and where has he gone?

"How about you show me around," Tracie says. "So I can get to know my new home."

I grin without covering my mouth when she says that.

Tracie wants to start downstairs where they held the meeting about her, so I lead her into the Sanctuary. The chairs make a half circle on the paisley carpet, around a table with a microphone hooked up to a taping machine.

"It was the TV lounge," I tell her, "back when this was a hotel and not the C.P.—I mean, Common Purse. See?" I finger the cable cords that come out of the wall in a spidery spray. "The TV connected here, and a satellite dish used to sit on the roof."

"What's the microphone for?"

"Leonard tapes his sermons for Christian radio on Sundays." I look at her sideways. "Leonard's my law-father, the one with the moustache. He does the talking."

"He's your daddy?"

I nod.

"Why don't you call him 'Daddy'?"

"There's nothing special about family ties. We're all brother and sister in the Lord."

Tracie taps on the button that makes the microphone record Leonard's voice when the machine is on. "That's nutty," she says.

I suddenly worry that she'll leave, thinking we're unnatural. But she smiles and clomps in her black boots to the little table in the back where I do my home school.

"But I guess that makes us sisters, Omi Ruth."

Okay, she'll stay by me, I know it. She's easy for me to talk to, like Loomis's North.

"So who's the younger man? The skinny one with the wire glasses. Looks about thirty."

"That's Jude. He's the cook and the gardener. He has books and books of poems that he reads at night, or the Bible sometimes." We're walking into the hallway now, and I point to

Jude's room across from the kitchen where she's already been. "He's close to tears most of the time, especially at the start of things, like a meal or a sermon or something pretty that's written. It's like he's already sad it will end." I've never said this about Jude before, yet it's true and I'm Miss Omi, I'm a chatty-box. "We take turns helping Jude with the dishes and meal cleanup."

"That so?" Tracie's looking at the closed door that leads to my brother Wood's room. A room I know is swept empty.

"No one in there," I say. "Or in this one," pointing to the room on the left, closest to the front door of the house that opens to the tiny stoop and Tyrone Road.

"So they rent these?" she asks.

"Old Loomis's napping in this one." I rush down the hall and tap Loomis's closed door next to Jude's, before some tears can sneak out and startle my desert-eyes. "And a half bath that's broken in the corner. That's all the downstairs, but I can take you out back."

"Slow down there, girl."

"I'll show you Jude's garden barrels." I'm moving toward the back screen door. I'm a chatty-box that has shut her lid. I chase my unwelcome tears back into my head as Odell's motorcycle roars up the alley. "Buey boys are next door," I say. "You coming?" I don't turn to look for her, but I hear her boots.

I'm down the steps where Spencer Frye hasn't left a flower in a jar beside the eggs for a week now. I weave around the barrels, a red bell pepper coming on, big and swollen. The sun hits me like I'm a mole breaking ground, since I haven't left the house for so long. Vaughn's there smoking a cigarette on his back steps in his blue work shirt. It's unsnapped so his chest is showing. He is like a shock.

"Oh me, oh my," says Vaughn softly to me. We haven't spoken this whole month, but I've glimpsed him through the sheer curtains upstairs when his black shade goes up. I know Tracie follows me because I watch his eyes watch her. I know he likes her perfect curls and slender legs and I don't know what else.

"Tracie Casteel, this is Vaughn Buey. Tracie's going to be staying with us."

"Is that right?" Vaughn blows smoke then crushes out his cigarette on the stone steps. "Pleased to meet you, Tracie Casteel."

"You too," she says, beside me now, but she's not paying attention. She turns to look at my unfinished mosaic.

Odell comes around the corner with black stains all over his work shirt that's like Vaughn's, with a sewn name patch, only dark red.

"Thought your lazy ass'd still be in bed," Odell says to Vaughn, like I'm not even standing there. Then he notices Tracie. "Excuse me," he says. Odell has a nasty beard on his chin and he's missing a front tooth—from a fight, Vaughn told me. "And who is this in our backyard?"

"Tracie, this is Odell," I say quietly, mad.

"Hey, Tracie," Odell says. He taps the bill of his cap that has Ripper on it in big letters, from the cinder-block place where he works. His sleeves are rolled up to show the dark ink tattoos on his forearm. Dragon-snake. A stupid pierced heart.

"Hi there," Tracie murmurs without looking his way. She walks around the barrels of plants, right up to my mosaic wall and touches it, so gently, like to see whether it's real.

Odell snorts.

"You did this, Omi Ruth, mmhmm?" She traces the trough between pieces where the grout would go if I finished it.

"She's a real Picasso," says Odell.

"What do you know about Picasso, dipshit?" Vaughn knocks his brother's hat from his head.

"Fuck off."

"You fuck off."

"Button your shirt, faggot." Odell grabs his hat and kicks gravel, going inside without saying good-bye. The duct tape curls off from where the door screen is torn.

"Omi's got some goddamn talent," Vaughn calls after Odell, and maybe over to Tracie, too. He fingers a front snap on his shirt. "I better get going. Got some stuff before work. You take care. Both of you." He says both, but it's Tracie's figure he watches before he walks around the corner where Odell just came from. Tracie hasn't stepped away from my mosaic.

"It's really nothing," I say, and I go back into the kitchen before she can say it's something. I know I'm being as rude as Odell. I stand with both hands on the kitchen table, holding me steady. Right now I long for a zinnia in a jar from Spencer who's forgotten about me. I hear the screen door open and shut and she's there, not angry or put out, though I sense the smoothness of her sorrowful curve, which she has told me nothing about.

"Wanna show me more of the upstairs?" Tracie doesn't ask anything else about the mosaic work, but I feel obliged.

"That's why I'm too pale," I say. "I used to work on it every sunny day, with broken saucers and things, in its own pattern. The sun was tanning me."

"I'm no stranger, Omi," she says to me, and it's somehow the perfect thing to say.

She follows me up the stairs this time, tapping the banister in a nice rhythm. Vaughn's exhaust pipes blow by through the alley.

"Those hoodlums live there alone?" she asks.

"No, their law-mother lives with them, Chastity Buey. She works odd hours at the diner, but you'll meet her. Vaughn's alright." I think of him and me and that hickory tree and his black shade and how he's never said before that I have talent. "Odell's the hoodlum. It's because they have different law-fathers. I never knew them since Chastity never married, but Odell's must have been a mean dimwit."

Tracie laughs behind me.

"What's funny?"

"Boys got different daddies she never married, with a name like Chastity? Too funny, mmhmm?"

I'm awake, but I don't answer. I start by pointing down the hallway toward the six-legged star. "Morse and Sue Calhoun at the very end. Morse is at the RV plant, but you saw Sue this morning. She's my home-school teacher."

"The one with her hair pinned up, or the mousy one with the straight bowl cut?"

Now I do laugh a little. "The mousy one. The other is Carson, my law-mother."

"So that's your mama." Tracie looks thoughtful. "Looks a little lonely, don't you think? Never would've guessed who was married to who."

"That's her and Leonard's room. And this next one's empty, beside us." I wonder, is it true Carson is lonely? What has it been like for her, for Leonard, to have no Wood? I do not know, I do not care. You're not allowed your own loneliness in a fellowship of all things in common. She's a stiff kind of lonely.

"Any other kids around?" Tracie's dancing a little, like she has to pee.

"Lucy Calhoun used to be, but she was older than me and

had straight hair and hated it here. These are all her clothes." I tug at the bottom of my too-small blouse. I don't want to tell Tracie about the lump, but out it comes. "Lucy had a lump in her breast for two years till her aunt Nancy took her away to the doctors. Then Nancy got her married, with two girls, then divorced, too, which about killed Morse and Sue." I know she has to pee, but I have to keep talking, saying things I didn't know I was thinking. "We're dying out like the seals. Soon no one will remember us and how we live here and what kinds of things we like to do. No one even marks our graves." I'm talking fast. "There's an old *National Geographic* on endangered species, and it showed the baby seals that got hunted too much. Like from the 1970s, I think. We're dying out like them, only not because lots of people come hunting for us, but because no one does. But this is Indiana. I mean, I've never seen the ocean or a baby seal, and maybe I won't get to if they die out. I keep searching new magazines to find out if they made it, but it never says." Talking too fast. I slow down my breath. Baby seals have black-pearl eyes looking up at you.

"Well, I'm here, mmhmm?"

I look at her, and it's true. She walked clear from her valley that's dark before it's dark, then clear from Detroit where there was no valley but the one they made up between the tracks and the river.

"And you ain't dying yet," she says. "And neither am I. But, girl, I have got to take a piss. I'm surprised this child let me wait this long." She shuts the bathroom door behind her, then peeks out. "This door lock?"

I wag my head.

"Well, keep an eye out then."

And I'm alone in the hallway. With my own loud heartbeat. I hear Tracie pee like a cow—what a stream!—then she sighs. I'm laughing at her when she comes out.

"Go on and snicker. You just wait till your bladder gets squished like a water balloon." She's not angry, I can tell.

"So," says Tracie to me, "just this last room in the corner."

I look at the crystal knob on the door that leads to Loomis's North. "Yes," I say, going somber and a little proud. But I'm not sure I want to take her in there. No one goes in but me and Jayne and Regina. What will happen if Tracie walks in with those boots and speaks with her Coal Lick voice? Will she understand him, how he needs me? How this is the room where time slows and almost stops, and hardly anything changes? I know Jayne and Regina have gone for the day and he lies there alone with the *click whirr, hiss hmm.* I put my finger to my lips to say shh. "He's sleeping."

"Who?" she whispers.

I turn the lovely knob and enter in, her boot-steps behind me. Then the breathing machine is all the noise there is, which means her boots have stopped in the doorway, not following me to his bed rail. The leaning bed slats by the window are gone, so Jude must have already found a mattress to go with the frame and set it up in my room for her.

"We should just let him sleep, Omi." She sees him lying there so softly, she doesn't want to be in here.

I touch below his elbow-bend to check for redness around the IV strap. It needs some Vaseline. How simple I am, I suddenly think. How simple and old to be a nurse for somebody held in between living and dying.

"You help take care of him?"

"Everyone's doing something that has fallen to her to do." I'm saying what Jayne has said to me. "He is what's fallen to me."

"You know, that Vaughn boy likes you." She says it a little louder than a whisper, like to get my attention, right in that room with Loomis's North. It's not true and I wish she hadn't said it. All I feel is sorrow and heaviness, for I know, right now, that it is this hush-man I love. My silent silver-white who asks nothing of me but the simplest of things. He does not ask me to be pretty, he does not roar up and down the alley like Vaughn or stand close to me with all earthiness and heat like Spencer that time when the shed walls pressed in close, he does not say to sweep aside Wood's soul that flutters in me with sharp wings or to shove out of my hermit-crab shell.

"Think I'll lay down for a bit," Tracie says, already retreating into the hallway to leave me here because she can tell. I turn and she's gone, which tears me in two. What is it she will ask of me? Why has she come? I lean close to his paper skin.

"I love you," I say. It is the first time I've said it. The first time I've understood it, or let myself think it without feeling it's wrong. I know I'm strange to feel this for him.

"But I'm not a stranger," I say. I take the little sponge on the windowsill and moisten his mouth. I dab a little Vaseline on his lips and on his arm where the tube goes in. I kiss his head so gently, snow on moss. What else could it mean to love someone except to not be afraid of him? I am still still beside his frail self.

But then I follow her fast, into our Big Top room where, sure enough, Jude has made up her bed with the matching blue and white gingham bed spread that used to be Lucy's. I'm relieved that Tracie has flopped herself down on the bed. She has kicked off her boots.

That night we have another prayer circle planned for the Sanctuary. Not a circle of welcome for Tracie, but a circle to bathe Loomis's North in our prayers. It's the third one Jude has asked Leonard for, on behalf of Loomis because she's too weak to climb the stairs to even see the man she's married to. Jude thinks that, even with her failing mind, she can feel connected to her North through prayer. Even though Jude is the one to use *brother* and *sister* with all our names, it's him who wants most for family ties to matter, which puzzles me.

Sue knocks on our door. Tracie has slept for hours—even slept through supper—and has long ago removed her green leggings, so it's just her bare legs and small flash of underwear greeting Sue as she peeks in.

"Oh," says Sue, mousy indeed. She whisks herself away then comes back with her ratty lavender bathrobe. "You can wear this, Miss Casteel. It's time for the prayer circle, girls."

Tracie squints and stretches. We're both reluctant to get up— her because she has walked all the way here from Detroit, and me because I've been looking and looking at the magazine that I hid in the folds of the dirty sheets, which I forgot to put in the wash. If I hadn't outgrown collage-making, the photos would make the finest, most beautiful collage, one that I would never dare show to anyone.

Leonard seems displeased by what Tracie's wearing, or maybe by her being here at all. He strokes the edges of his neat moustache and sits beside Morse who waits for Leonard to introduce her, which he is not about to do.

"Morse Calhoun," I say, "this is Tracie Casteel," and Morse nods his wide flattop head. Tracie murmurs her "hi there" and yawns a big yawn, lifts her bleached hair from her neck so the hoop earrings dangle free for a moment. We're all here but Jude. Then he walks in. He has put on pressed blue pants and a white linen shirt. Where did he get those? He usually wears his garden jeans all summer, dirt at the knees, even on Sundays, and sometimes the canvas apron from the kitchen, too. He has combed his hair to the side. I've never noticed Jude's hair. It's thin and light brown and tonight its wave shows up in a handsome way. Leonard does not lose his look of displeasure.

It's not that late but Loomis already wears her nightgown, flannel even in summer. She holds a cup of warmed milk that she sips loudly, which makes me spiteful toward her. She would never do that during a taping of one of Leonard's sermons.

This will be the same as the other circles: holding hands in one accord, bowing heads and listening to Leonard ask God's mercy and ask God's will—he asks for God's sparing hand but then tells God to go on and do whatever he pleases. If I were God, I'd be confused about what it is Leonard's after.

"We know Northrop is knocking on your door," he prays now—a little scornful, I think, even when he addresses God— "and we ask entry when it's time. But have mercy on us, O Lord, for we are earthly beings that have felt the sting of death. Forgive us our grasping hands. We thank you for the gift of Northrop's presence until you call him home."

Then I tune it out because I don't want to be forgiven for my hands and I don't want Loomis's North called anyplace elsewhere. I do what I've done during the other night-prayers: I close my eyes and search my photographic memory for what everybody's shoes look like, then I peek out to check whether I'm right. Maybe it's as disrespectful as Loomis drinking her milk like a stray cat, but I don't think so because I know him. I touch him and swaddle him up in clean sheets. Leonard prays for a ghost, for a hollow husk, but he's the husk—Leonard. I'm the one that handles Loomis's North, and, for a month now, I've taken care with the light showing up through his skin, light shining through all his vast, uncobwebbed insides.

Besides, I'd rather not pray at all, for I'm not on the best terms with God. He's got two counts against him: first, not protecting my Wood in the head-on and second, letting them put Wood's body in the belly of the earth while he still wore his chore pants, with hardly a scrap up top to remember him by. Last time I prayed, it was for cold cash, a whole bucket of fifty-dollar bills, to buy a beautiful grave marker. And God has yet to deliver.

Carson's shoes are the cheap white canvas, I know, from the dollar store. She thinks they look like a nurse's shoes. I peek, and I'm right. Morse will still have his steel toes on, plaster creased in around the sockets for the laces—yes, Sue in thin sandals, Leonard in loafers, Loomis in soft slippers that show her sock foot in front. I think: hole in the sock toe, and I'm right on that, too. But which will Jude have on? I scroll through his few pairs and choose the black, which is right, though I did not foresee the shine on them. And Tracie? Did she pull her boots back on to come downstairs? Their laces crisscrossed and still too long so wrapped once around her slender legs? Thick soles that could stamp out a fire? I peek. No boots, just barefoot with a surprise: toenails painted the pink of her sweater. Now I'm out of feet, but Leonard drones on, so I just study the old paisley carpet, then close my eyes and imagine the shoes that walked here back when this was a hotel and people watched late-night TV and tried to not be lonely in a place full of strangers.

Amens, like murmurs in a tin can on a string, and Loomis is the first to shuffle out. Everybody goes till it's me and Tracie and Jude. He's straightening the chairs that don't need straightening. Tracie stands and hugs herself inside Sue's lavender robe with dark purple cording at the cuffs. Seems to me that her sad curve has gone deeper and more weary.

"Is your room fixed up alright?" Jude asks her without looking away from the chair he nudges into some proper place.

"It's fine, Mr. Jude. I thank you." She gives her funny nod and curtsy again, but less teasing this time and more sad, which makes me think for the first time that she had nowhere else to go but here. He blushes after she says his name.

"Just Jude, Sister Tracie."

"That's fine," she says, tired.

I head out the door and am not sure she's with me since she wears no boots to clomp, but I need to go, to say good-night to Loomis's North who's nearly drowning now in the pool of our prayers. At the top of the stairs, I look back and she's not coming yet. In my room, I slip the *National Geographic* out from under my pillow, then slip myself through his door and don't switch on the light.

I'm shy because of my kiss from before, but only for a moment. In one hand I hold the magazine to show him, and with my other hand I hold his bed rail like I've held a wire handle of a pail and like I've held the one side, then both sides, of the pliers I have used to bust up saucers for my mosaic wall. There's moonlight only.

"She's diving for abalone," I say, letting loose of the rail to point to the naked woman on the cover, to her feet up in the air and her one hand about to steal her woven basket from the rowboat. I flip to the feature article inside. "It's a shellfish in icy water in Japan. Ama divers, they're called, see?" I show him, not a photo, but an old painting of the women's white bodies in the

66

sea, some with scarves on their hair, some with it streaming behind them in dark black ink. Some wringing it dry while sitting
on a wide stone on the shore, women in fine robes laid open
down the middle like Vaughn's work shirts. Japanese letters fill
the corner of the painting like a beetle's careful footprints. Then
a photo, next page, five women dressing around a fire. Their
breasts fall loose, with a shadow smiling underneath each one.

"They dive alone but not alone. They whistle to each other,
like shorebirds. They've done it for two thousand years—can
you imagine?" I look at his eyelids and I know he can imagine,
right up to the end. I tell him how sometimes they come up
with pearls and red seaweed and sea snails. Some of the women
are old, even though there are sharks and jellyfish and things.
Sometimes they wear wetsuits nowadays, with all the gear, but
some still like to go bare skinned, without even oxygen machines, like the one he has.

When I lay on my bed earlier, reading on my belly as Tracie slept, I tried to see how long I could hold my breath—I
counted only nineteen seconds, but the divers go for way over a
minute. I lay there thinking how I would show Loomis's North
these pictures tonight, and I felt a slow rubbing between my
legs though nothing rubbed me. It wasn't my Always pad. It
was like vibration, like being inside a vibrating sound until it
was inside me. My part down there opened and shut, and I
gasped and looked over at Tracie, thankful she was still out
cold. I reached down, before I knew what I was doing, and un-
buttoned my jean cutoffs to feel for it. But Tracie made a sound
and rolled over, and my hand flew up to touch my hair.

I feel the weak echo of it now, between my legs, just a tingle
at his bedside. I flush hot in my face because I wish so badly to
feel it all the way, like before, that full shudder.

I whisper: "Listen now to what the ama diver says. 'I hear the sea flood my body, I hear the sunlight pierce the water, the sound of fish, so silent but so noisy.'" I do feel a soft rush. "You are brave like her," I say to him. "The place where you are." I stroke his white eyebrow so the hairs smooth into an arc; I wet his lips with the little sponge so he feels no thirst. "What do you hear in there, mmhmm?" I'm talking like Tracie, seeing whether he's awake.

I close the *National Geographic* that's plenty creased on its yellow spine. Tracie must be in her bed by now, beside mine. I'll wait awhile before I leave his side. I would like to sleep here in this quiet room, but I know I can't. Even Jayne would frown. But I tell him, "Don't worry, I have a sister here now. I sleep alone but not alone." I don't kiss him this time, but I place my warm red cheek on his cool one and listen to his underwater light.

HOME ECONOMICS

In a week, here comes Nancy Calhoun with an armful of books and a zippered canvas sack.

Tracie and I were cooling on the front stoop of Solomon's Porch, facing Tyrone Road. I still don't go up the block, or down the alley, but she gets me out on the stoop most days. I spotted Nancy's green station wagon driving up, and her waving like wild; she slowed and took a long hungry look at Tracie in her stretchy skirt, her hairless legs, and her light white sweater that set off her tanned skin.

"Yes, my dear, you are aglow!" said Nancy out her car window, and she pulled into the alley to park. Tracie took one look at me and her laughter triggered mine. We laughed loud and long till finally Nancy swooped in behind us at the front door and clucked and said, "Come on, girls." We were laughing so hard we could hardly stand.

Now we sit somberly at the back table in the Sanctuary reading the covers of Nancy's books. Home school's out for the summer, but I guess home ec is still in session. And there's no sewing kit in sight; we have only one subject.

"Pregnancy!" Nancy says, smiling and making a sunrise-arc

with her hands that then swing down at her sides, two tongues in the bells of her ruffly sleeves. I'm glad I'm not the only one for Nancy to moon over now.

The stoop-sitting is Tracie's favorite part of the day. She said it was a waste to live in a place called a "porch" and never sit out on one. She said our stoop reminded her of Detroit, and of Coal Lick before that, when people sat out front in the evening and drank sweet tea and hollered their news to each other, or sat silently and counted the lightning bugs. I never sat out by Tyrone Road—because of the dusty traffic, but also because the black boys who lived in the apartments next door walked that way and I was told to be careful about them. I didn't tell Tracie that though.

"Let's sit out front," she said her second day here, "I'm feeling closed in," and then we did it every evening, just me and her. It was something I liked right away, despite my nervousness about the boys, because I got to watch the comings and goings of Dunlap, and for some reason it felt good to see that the town had kept in motion while I'd been hiding away inside. We could see clear to the traffic light where Tyrone crossed Jackson, where Chalkers pool hall was, and bars Odell went to. The other way, we could see the hardware sign and the trucks of the men picking up tools and rope and whatever, till closing.

One evening Tracie offered to work on my hair out there.

"Mama'd do my hair on the front stoop," she said, "when she was sober."

"What do you mean 'sober'?"

"I mean when she wasn't drunk." Tracie sat me on the lower step and herself on the higher, a leg on each side of me, purple leggings tucked into her sure boots. She unscrewed the lid from her tin of pomade.

"She drank beer?" I asked. Odell drank beer from can after can.

"She drank anything."

Tracie's sad shoulders, somewhere behind me, tried to un-curve, I could tell. She started at the wild tips of my hair and worked her way up, separating out the coils. Somewhere be-hind me, a baby moved or didn't move in her middle.

"Do you want to be a law-mother?" I asked, for she'd never said how she felt about it, one way or the other.

"Law ain't got nothing to do with it, Omi Ruth. But, yes, I do. It's a girl, I think, I just got a feeling. I wanna carry her around and show her things."

"You want to oil her hair?"

"I do. Mama wanted six babies, but just got me before Daddy took off. It's what made her sad enough to drink herself blind. I was just a reminder of the five she never had." Tracie laughed an unnatural laugh. "After he left, she beat me every little bit. I reminded her of him, too. I had his hair and she didn't know how to tame it. Once, when she was at work, I bleached it blond with Clorox so it would look like hers—hers was natural, so blond it was white, and straight and thin as corn silk. Nothing in the world that pretty, mmhmm?"

Tracie's talk was that lazy smooth talk, and it lulled me al-most to sleep as she worked the pomade into my hair. The po-made had a chemical smell with a mint-tea scent to cover it up.

"Tracie," I whispered, "how are you so sweet after all that?"

"I don't know how sweet I am, Omi Ruth. I got a mean streak too. And it wasn't all bad either." She stuck all her fin-gers into the thicket of my hair and massaged at the roots. It was pure delight. "If you could've known my daddy and how he and Mama would dance around in that shoebox-kitchen we had. They wore out the floor. I'd sing for them. Daddy wanted me to be a famous gospel singer." And she surprised me with a little tune, like a low-toned bird, crooning softly with no words, just sounds.

"Oh, Tracie, I can't sing," I said. "None of us can."

She kept at it. I felt the song in her fingers slick with pomade.

"Why did he leave?" I asked.

"Who? Daddy? Mmm. I don't know. Things went wrong. He got sad, he and Mama fought. But before he left, he signed me up for voice lessons at the civic center and paid for them too. The lessons just about ruined me but he never knew that. The civic ladies tried to take the sandpaper out of my voice, but that gritty part's the part he loved. That's the part that makes you a gospel singer fit for radio."

I waited for more song, but it didn't come.

"I was going to be on radio," she said and she stopped her hands in my hair.

I turned around to face her. "My brother wanted to be on radio. He was shy but he did voices, like a cowboy voice and a newscaster, and a real funny prim-lady voice."

"That so."

"I had a brother who died." It was the first time I'd admitted it to her. "Woodrun. That's his name."

"I know, Omi. Jude told me. I know he slept in that room beside Loomis. I know you miss him."

I spun back around toward Tyrone Road and said, "Tell me more about your gospel songs." I focused my mind hard on the singled-out curls, on the ends of their almost-pretty spirals.

Right then a boy turned the corner and walked toward us down Tyrone. I watched him kick a can on the sidewalk. I went stiff, but Tracie dipped more pomade and started a new strand. He was tall and his skin was dark black, his black hair cropped close to his head. He dipped his body a little with each step, slowly, smoothly. I watched his bright white shoes and nothing else.

"Evening," I heard him say.

"Evening," Tracie said back.

I started thinking up a reason why we'd need to go inside. Supper, a sinkful of dishes, our turn to help Jude water the barrel garden.

"A real nice evening," Tracie said, "and just look at her curls."

"Nice," said the boy. I looked up from his shoes for long enough to see him smile. "Reagan," pointing to himself. "I have two little sisters doing hair every night over there," pointing toward the apartments.

I didn't know that any girls lived there.

Morse Calhoun's truck drove up to us then, home from the plant. He's the only one in the C.P. with a vehicle. He let the truck idle and rolled down his window. "Go on, skedaddle," Morse said. We all three looked at him. "Go on."

Tracie stood up fast, and she forgot that she held me in a tangle.

"Ouch!" I yelled.

"Not you, Miss Casteel." Morse waved his hand at Reagan like he might wave off an alley dog. Reagan didn't say a word, just walked. He walked as slowly and smoothly as he had before, not hurrying, even though Morse followed him just as slowly in his truck, all the way to the door, before turning down the alley.

Next thing I knew, Tracie was screwing on the lid to her tin of pomade, tighter and tighter, like she wanted to make sure nobody would be able to get it off again. I rubbed my head where she'd pulled. I wanted to tell her more about Wood, and about my plan to get a big, beautiful grave marker, and to ask what markers were put up for her law-parents when they'd died. But then Tracie said: "Fucking flattopped bigot."

I about jumped off the stoop to hear her talk like that, like Vaughn and Odell. This girl who wanted to sing gospel and who carried a baby inside her every step she took. This girl whose fingers smeared love into my hair.

The first book Nancy holds up is *Midwifery and the Modern Woman*.

"My bible," she says.

Then, it's *Your Amazing Newborn* and *Bonding* and *The Complete Book of Breastfeeding*. I think she's brought the whole library from her South Bend clinic.

"But I have two copies of this one." She tries to hand each of us a thick paperback, *Pregnancy and Childbirth: The Complete Guide*. We're showing her with our folded arms that we don't need her sunshiny instruction, but she lands a book into each of our laps. "An absolute must for a mother-to-be"—then Nancy looks at me—"and for her little helper." A huge-bellied woman with perfect hair poofed in a headband looks out wishfully from the cover; she smiles right into the slanted letters: "Over 1,000,000 Copies Sold!"

"We know Naomi is a good little helper, don't we?" Nancy pats Tracie's wrist.

Tracie snorts, but she stares at the woman on the book's cover. I wonder whether she's anxious about getting that big.

I see what's going on right away. I remember Nancy shouting at Leonard just after Wood died, when I was helping Jayne upstairs. She shouldn't be near a dying person, Nancy had said, now of all times. *Now*, which was the Time of Loss, and it's still that time. No doubt Carson or Sue has told her of my hours and hours helping with Loomis's North, and Nancy has thought me oppressed, in the clutches of a cult. She wants to save me by making me apprentice midwife.

Well, I'm not having it.

I stand up, about to get bold and to tell Tracie to come on, it's summer, and home ec is canceled, when I see that Tracie has found something in the book and her eyes are glued there, wide. I look where she's looking. Nancy's face bobs up beside mine like a shiny apple.

It's a black-and-white drawing of a baby in a womb, inside a woman's profile going from breast to thigh. Tracie doesn't blink. "Second trimester," it reads beneath the drawing. The baby is a bat, hanging upside down with something coming out its belly and attaching to the womb's wall. It's smooshed tight in there, its bald head like one of Jude's fat horticulture beans ready to be shelled out.

Nancy's breath smells like cinnamon candy. "See there? It's a must read, Tracie. This book will help you bring your sweet baby down that long passage home."

Then Tracie laughs and breaks her gaze, which gives me some relief, though she wipes a tear off her cheek, secretly but I see it.

Nancy takes the book and flips to a later section. "You need to make sure you get the nutrients you need. Do not, and I mean *do not*, skimp on your iron and calcium. Here you are." She unzips her canvas bag and pulls out a big plastic bottle. "I've brought you your prenatals. This should get you through a few months. And your protein—don't worry, I'm giving some Xeroxes to Jude for your dietary needs, which you do *not*, Omi dear, need to mention to your tightwad father." She sniffs and flips to a chart. "And see this? This, my girl, is a list of the birth defects that come from not getting those nutrients. And a cleft palate is the least of them, take my word. Oh, what these eyes have seen." Big dramatic wave of her hand.

Tracie plays with her silver hoop earring, runs her finger round and round. I think of the baby stuck inside her without any room to turn or flip. At least, that's how the drawing made it look. Closed in, like in a little oval coffin. How does it breathe?

"These first chapters," Nancy goes on, "deal with the anatomy of reproduction and conception, which Naomi and I covered in our home economics course this spring, and I don't think you need much education on that, do you, dear?" She winks at Tracie. "So just skip ahead to chapters three through six for next Thursday—on the first and second trimesters and calculating your due date—I can help you with that. And your nutrient needs. Remember your nutrients," patting Tracie's wrist with each word. Nancy pulls her open canvas sack into her lap. She beams and pushes up her floppy sleeves. "Now. Tracie. I've brought you something very special. This is a humble collection of sundresses that I loan out to my mothers-to-be in summer. It can be a trial to think you're losing your beauty and your lithe young shape. But you *have* to remember how beautiful you are with a child in your womb. You need to think, 'I am the first ray of sunshine my child will see.' I loan out these dresses to remind you of your loveliness," and she starts pulling them out like they're sacred.

"No thank you, Miss Nancy," Tracie says.

Nancy's face sinks. "But look, they're quite lovely. Perfect for your size."

"I said no thank you."

"But you can't wear long-sleeved sweaters like that in this heat."

"No thank you." The last time, quiet.

I think one of the sheer green dresses is pretty, with a scooped back, and I want Tracie to take it. Maybe she's too proud. It's true that she always wears sweaters, here in late July. I think: I've never seen her take off one sweater to change to another. She must do it in the bathroom, which is funny since she's not one bit shy about changing her leggings and her underwear in front of me (she's got underwear to match all four colors of our Big Top room and more colors and lacy designs besides). And it's not her belly she's shy about; she's always lifting her sweater up to peek at her growing middle, with me able to see it all, even the line of dark hairs going down from her belly button. Maybe it's her arms or her back she wants to keep private, but why, I wonder.

Nancy is upset. This was to be her best gift. She clutches the canvas bag and turns her voice all business, no more ruffles. "Next Thursday then? Same time? Five p.m." Out from under the stack of books she pulls a binder she must use as a daybook for her appointments. She scribbles in it then closes it on the table and stuffs her lovely sundresses back into the bag without much care. Underneath the clear plastic on the cover of the binder is a photo collage that draws my eye.

Oh.

The second set of naked pictures I've seen. Photographs of what I think are real live births. I make sure Tracie's not looking, and she's not—she's trying to fold a dress for Nancy—because—I gawk—the women's legs are like wide-apart handles on a pair of pliers. The women are bloody and split open. Oh, how could that tiny blue baby be alive? When it makes the Long

Passage—that's how Nancy said it. The babies look dead, tiny arms slung every which way. I cover the binder fast with my copy of *The Complete Guide*, one of the million copies sold.

I tiptoe into our room that night—after I sat with Loomis's North a spell and told him about Nancy's meddling—and Tracie's got the pregnancy book like a tent over her face, reading in Sue's bathrobe. Her hair sprays all over the pillow and leaves her silver hoops unhassled; she never takes them out when she sleeps. One lovely knee sticks up, and the robe flaps open to show her underwear with tiny butterflies all over. The sides of the panties are thin as strings, barely there.

I want her to tell me a story about Detroit, about her friend who lost her leg to the train tracks, about the smell of rain in Coal Lick—stories she's told me before. But she's deep into chapters three through six. I want her old self that I've known for a whole week now, which has seemed like a year, ten years. I try to make myself into a chatty-box to get her going, but my lid won't open.

So I roll over and listen to her flip pages.

Till I hear another sound. It's something I've heard at other times, late in the night, but I usually end up thinking it's outside. A scrap between cats. Tonight I know it's in the house. Like a grunt, or something lower. And a rhythm.

"Well, well," Tracie says. "Glad *some*body's doing it in this house." She shuts her tent-book and drops the pretty, wishful woman face-first to the floor.

"Doing what?" I ask.

Tracie turns to me, leaning on her elbow. "Thought you covered that already with Miss Nancy Sunshine. You don't hear that?"

Grunting, I think is right. The lower is another sound, a voice, I realize. "Is that some*body*?" I hear it louder, a moan.

"That. Omi Ruth. Is the sound of two people going at it." She thumbs toward the green wall shared with the empty room. She whispers through a sly smile, "Your mama and daddy's having sex."

One louder moan, then quiet. My body is stiff as stone, and I could hear an ant crawl, I'm perched here listening so hard. I don't breathe.

Footsteps then, sounding hard, like Leonard's going down the stairs.

"He gets it done awful quick." She giggles a little.

I say nothing. I hear nothing else. I picture Carson lying in her bed, counting her bobby pins. Suddenly, she is a woman in the photo collage in Nancy's binder, she is bloody and split open, legs apart. "No," I say, "that's not true."

"What's wrong?" Tracie lets go of her smile. "Hey, it's okay. Be glad for it. It's a little bit of normal in this place."

I'm sitting up, shaking my head, saying no with my head, but shaking out the pictures too—that binder's photographs that bleed into a field of dead bodies. My mind reaches for other pictures, and it's the baby seal pleading help from me, a shark not in the picture but just outside it, and the white naked body diving for a last shellfish. Then Tracie is beside me.

"Hey," she says, with one hand on my head to still me. "What is it?" But I don't know what it is. The pictures loom too brightly, shark teeth and blood, tiny blue babies, Carson split wide, Tracie split wide, then the older picture of the soul's scared knees knocking together, and Loomis's North getting a bedsore on his left side, and—she shushes me, but I would like to cry.

"I know, Omi, it must seem strange to you. It can be a beautiful thing when two people want it."

I shake my head.

My head is in her lap and she strokes my forehead, strokes and strokes, with one hand then another, and talks softly. "You're a little young to think much about it, okay? But it's not a bad thing. People can make it dirty, the Buey boys maybe, or Odell at least. But it don't have to be. My mama never said much. Far as I know, she never did it with nobody else after Daddy left. We had a tiny house in Coal Lick, and I slept in the loft right above them. They couldn't help but share their sounds with me, but I didn't mind. She'd be quiet sometimes, and laugh sometimes, and he'd say, 'You're beautiful,' over and over." Tracie's hands feel like tree leaves in wind brushing my forehead. Brushing away one picture then another, and I calm. "I promised myself it'd be like that for me. And, let me tell you, I had to fight for it sometimes. Shouldn't be that way, but it is." Her voice gets as wishful as the guidebook woman's face. "Omi, here. Touch here." She puts my hand on her belly where the small rise is, right above the little butterflies. "Feel that?"

I feel the little hairs that grow below her bellybutton. I feel skin that's thick and safe for whatever's inside it.

"That can't come from something dirty, can it." Tracie's sad curve is a shawl around me. Somebody has lain with her and called her beautiful. He must have been gentle with her. He must have left her, too, like her daddy.

Tracie lies back on my bed and lays me down beside her so we're looking up into our Big Top. She starts telling me a story of a real circus she saw once by the river in Detroit. There was a girl on trapeze who flitted from one trapeze to the other, quick as a honey bee; she wore this silver sequins outfit, with feathers;

we waited for her to fall, Tracie says—we held our breath—but she never did.

I drift to sleep, and the only picture left in my head is a girl in silver and feather. And the only thing I hear when the story fades out is Tracie's soft singing in my bed, like my own live radio, the lightest sandpapery voice. She sleeps there beside me, with her robe flapped open, her legs loose.

She's up before me in the morning. I see her gingham bed spread rumpled, so she must have climbed into her own bed while I dreamed.

It's August before we know it, and we've got box fans fighting the heat from every window in Solomon's Porch. Tracie hasn't brought in the mail since that first day she showed up with her duffle bag, but after August 1, she starts checking it anxiously, watching for her government check.

She also starts waking up way earlier than me. I still make sure to sleep late, sometimes till ten, and Jayne has taken to knocking softly on my door to let me know it's time for my chores with Loomis's North. Tracie says she's up early because the baby won't let her sleep. It's not moving yet, even though the pregnancy book says she could feel it move at any time, but just the idea of it wakes her up, she says—the idea that it has, according to our guide, tiny eyelashes and tiny fingernails. "And its thoughts and feelings are so loud, they wake me up," says Tracie to me, half giddy.

One early morning, a light knock at the door, and I wake. It's still dark, so I know it's not Jayne. Tracie pops her head in and comes over to kneel at my bedside.

"Come on, sleepyhead," she whispers and jostles me till I sit up. "Some shy boy is asking for you downstairs. Come on. Says he got something for you. Kinda cute too." She smiles at me through my thick curtain of sleep. I roll toward the wall, but she grabs my bed sheet and pulls it back.

"Stop!" I say.

"Up you go, lazybones." Tracie grabs Sue's lavender robe from her bed—she's dressed in her sweater and leggings already—and holds it out for me. In my nightgown, I shove one heavy arm in a sleeve, then the other, grouchy. I follow her down the stairs to find Spencer Frye standing in the kitchen holding a dollar-store bag.

I stop fast in my tracks and feel my thicket of hair going all the wrong ways. I cover my mouth, but Tracie gently pulls my hand away, takes it in hers, and leads me into the kitchen. Spencer shoots a glance at me then looks at the linoleum. I can't believe I'm in this bathrobe. I quickly tie the belt that I've let hang. I haven't seen him since we carried pails brimming with fresh milk.

Tracie Casteel has disappeared.

"I have the eggs outside," says Spencer to me. "I have these for you." He holds out the sack, his arm stiff as a tree branch. I walk around the kitchen table and accept it without touching his hand.

"Radishes," he says.

I can't yet speak a word out loud. No light is on in the kitchen, so it's just the almost-sunrise light that falls on him from the windows. He's dressed funny, in jeans and a rock band T-shirt and white tennis shoes, like the ones Reagan wears when he walks by us most evenings now and waves but doesn't speak. Where is Spencer's white collared shirt?

"I came to tell you why I do not bring flowers for you now." He looks different but sounds the same, that formal voice.

For me. Then it's true those flowers had all been for me. Every strong-stemmed zinnia.

He says, "When I started my rumspringa year I chose to move off Father's farm. I moved in with some other boys who have bought a vehicle, but I still drive the buggy. I prefer it. I am wearing what I want. I am still working half-day for the Booths, but I work at Cindy Lane's Diner too. I bus tables." He puts his hands in his pockets like he's worn Levi's all his life. I wonder, does he work the same hours as Chastity Buey? Then the thought of the Bueys makes me ache in my chest bone, the thought of Vaughn. "I used to cut the flowers from Mother's kitchen garden before delivering the eggs each day." He looks guilty. His dark hair is longer than before, and he tosses his head to keep it from his eyes. "Mother said not to do it anymore. I think because she is not in favor of my choice to be like this. Out in the world."

I peek into the bag and look at my million radishes, all deep pink with sprouts of green at the tops.

"I am sorry," he says and steps toward me, close enough to touch the bag in my hands, which he does, and he grazes my fingers. "These I bought from Mrs. Booth who raises no flower garden. I want to give you flowers instead."

I remember that cheese-making shed, and I'm there again with the walls closing in and his blue eyes piercing me with icy heat. I can't help but hear my brother Wood calling to me then, "Omi Ruth!" from the tractor, for our quick getaway—I remember how I was torn in two and how I chose that day to fly to Wood. His call is so real I look over at the door to Wood's room and I see that it's open a crack, though it's never open, so it's like he's really in there.

"Do you not like it when I give you the flowers?" Spencer Frye says, and his tone is wavery. "Do you not like them?"

I open my mouth and, finally, I have a voice. "I love them," I say, looking at that barely open door, and I run out of the kitchen, up the stairs, holding tightly to my sack of radishes.

All day Tracie waits for me to tell her who is that shy boy with the odd offering. But my chatty-box lid is shut tight.

The next morning I wake up at the same still-dark hour, and I hear the black Amish buggy out the window, the horse hooves. I hear it come; I hear it sit there silently, as though waiting; then I hear it pull away. And I hear the fury of Vaughn's harsh exhaust when he comes off shift from the plant. I lie listening to every single thing in the world driving by outside without me. I stay in bed, but I can't fall back to sleep.

Finally, five days into August, Tracie's check comes in the mail. She rips into it, says, "Yes sir," signs the back and folds it in half. Jude is there watching her, wiping cucumber peels from his hands onto his canvas apron.

"I'm ready to dump it in," says Tracie, proud. I want to know how much the check is for, but she's not telling. "We're about to fatten up this Common Purse."

Jude beams at her, open faced like a child.

"So where's it go?" she asks him.

Jude leads Tracie and me into the Sanctuary where Leonard sits with his sermon-writing face on. He does that machine-like turn, clearly displeased to be interrupted by Tracie Casteel.

"Sister Tracie would like to give freely of her money gift," Jude says to Leonard, as if he's even prouder than Tracie is.

"Right at this very moment?" Leonard mutters.

"Is it not fitting, Brother Leonard, to receive whenever the Lord chooses to give?"

Leonard raises his eyebrows at Jude and sets down his pencil. "Summon the witnesses, I suppose."

Loomis is napping, so we let her be. Morse is at the plant since it's not even noon yet, but Tracie fetches Sue who's watering the barrels out back. Sue slips off her muddy sandals outside the Sanctuary and enters barefoot.

"Where's Carson?" Tracie asks with plain eagerness.

"I believe Sister Carson is completing some correspondence work," says Jude. "In the empty room upstairs."

"I'll go," I say, and I find myself doing two stairs at a time, as eager as Tracie for her Giving Without Compulsion, the most holy act in the C.P. But, once upstairs, I know I'm eager for another reason too: to summon Carson myself. I have hardly recognized her these days, for reasons I don't quite understand. It's partly that night of grunting and moaning; it's partly the chapter in the *Complete Guide* that I read on breastfeeding and I asked her, did she breastfeed me, and she said no, it was too crude. It's partly her thinning face, like she is hungrier and hungrier.

Now I slow down at the top of the stairs.

For it's partly something even more difficult to describe: her love for order. Everything—from her pinned-up hair to the number of pages of correspondence schoolwork she does each day—it's always in perfect order. She never falls apart into a pile of loose feathers. Sadness, it seems to me, has never touched her, like it touched Tracie's mama, or not just *touched*, but slapped and wrestled Tracie's mama to the ground. Carson likes her neat nursing books and note-taking, but she does not like to touch people the way I touch Loomis's North like a real nurse. She could never change his sheets and colostomy. When

I started helping Jayne and Regina care for him, Carson all but quit speaking to me. She knows, I think, that I'm doing what she can't. Maybe I want to ask her why. Maybe I want to tell her it's okay.

I walk down the hallway to the room she's in. I picture her desk with papers on it, and I want to be a wind to blow the papers all in a mess. I burst into the room and call out "Carson" but think "Mama." There she is—she whips her head and body to the side so I see her stiff profile. Her left hand out in front of her, holding something. She doesn't answer, so I walk closer. She holds a small photograph of my brother Wood. Her law-son. He is in his blue graduation cap that the home school ordered, with a little golden tassel. Down the cap and tassel fall as she lets the photo slip from her fingers.

She closes the book neatly on the desk and nudges her papers into a perfect stack. She rises and leaves me, going down the stairs without a word. The little tassel brushes the floor, Wood's hazel eyes that are my hazel eyes gaze into the floor, and I see only the white back of the wallet-size picture. I leave it for her, even though I want to take it, and I follow her down the stairs.

Jude has his Bible with the golden-edge pages open when I walk back into the Sanctuary. He stands alert, still in his peeling-speckled apron. Carson studies the paisley swirls. Leonard removes the lamp beside his microphone table from the tall wooden box it sits on. It looks like a nightstand, but without the lamp you can see the small knob on the top of the box. He pulls it up, and up comes the lid with a popping sound. I notice how this skinny little box could topple any minute, could be emptied by a careful thief at any time, this box that holds the contents of our Common Purse. I always thought it should be a cloth purse with a drawstring, like a marble bag, but, no, it's this box. Up till now, in my memory, it's only been Morse who's had a check to give, and Loomis her SSI, but those are just regular deposits, made without ceremony. It's only a member's first giving we have to witness.

Tracie has her fist on her hip; she lets it drop and clomps over in her boots to make her offering.

"First the reading," says Leonard, holding up his hand, like he's protecting the contents from her, like he's not too sure she won't pluck out what's inside and make a run for it. Her fist goes firmly back to her hip. He can't rain on her parade; she's pleased today.

"And they continued steadfastly in the apostles' doctrine and fellowship," reads Jude from the Book of Acts, with his crystal-clear voice already dribbled with tears. "In the breaking of bread, and in prayers. Then fear came upon every soul, and many wonders and signs were done through the apostles. Now all who believed were together, and had all things in common, and sold their possessions and goods, and divided them among all. As. Anyone. Had. Need." He holds out the end of things when he reads, trying to make them last. I can't help but see Wood's blue cap and gold tassel in my mind; I'm careful to piece together his face under the cap because lately his features have blurred for me, though never his eyes. He had need, I think to myself. He had need for a prettier, grander marker for where he lies in the dirt by that chain-link fence, by the Wendy's parking lot with Frosty cups blowing all over, and burger foils.

"Now can I?" Tracie asks, cocking her head to the side. Silver hoop teasing Leonard with its glint.

Leonard nods to her and backs away from the box. "Bless this offering, O Lord," he says. "To your glory and good work."

"Bless this 3,462 dollars, good Lord!" Tracie all but shouts it, and I see Leonard's eyes turn to saucers. Nobody thought it was that much. "And bless this child who's coming home, not too soon, but she's on her way." She rubs her belly and drops the folded check into the wooden box. "Amen."

Amens—those murmurs in a tin can.

"Amen!" I'm the only one that says it loud and clear, and I grin at Tracie. For, just like that, she has answered my prayer. Oh, it's plain as day. I'm jittery inside with delight, and some of the jitters must be my brother's soul moving in me. Once that check is cashed, oh, I will take just a little—no one will miss it, not even Tightwad Leonard Wincott—just a tiny bit, but enough to buy that big beautiful marker for Wood's grave. Yes, indeed. Tracie Casteel is my answer to prayer. She grins back at me like she knows it.

I'm at his metal bed rail right after Tracie's giving. It's almost noon, so Jayne and Regina are on lunch. I sit on the chair but lean most of my weight over the rail so that the mole by my mouth and some strands of my long hair, recently pieced out with pomade again, rest on his still hand. I don't bare my crooked teeth, and then I do. I don't think he minds. And maybe they're not as ugly as I think. My eyes look clearly into his face.

"If you could see me," I say, "you would see these eyes. They are the same as my brother's. So you would see him, too." I close my eyes and back a little off his hand. To my eyelid, I lift his fingertips to touch. They're paintbrushes, they're how he sees out from his place between living and dying. I move them to my eyebrow, to my temple, my cheek. I place one of my hands over my tender chest and feel there just for a moment. And another moment.

"I have to steal," I admit to him. "But it's not really stealing because the money is there as anyone has need. And we have need."

Today I choose to stop calling him Loomis's North. For what makes him hers? Besides the fact that they're married? What is it to be married? It's bed sharing, but they don't do that. And I'm the one who makes his bed, so you might say I do more of the sharing. Like Jude, I want the ties to matter, but not before I choose which ties. I don't know why Loomis has brought him here.

"But you're my North, too," I whisper.

Click whirr, hiss hmm.

No other sound in this room but his fingertips seeing and seeing me. Until: the whistle blows the noon hour at the RV plant, loud and mournful. I sit up. The sound is soon over, but it keeps coming from someplace. It comes out from under his pillow and hair, or out from his nostrils and oxygen tubing, or his line of lips. It sounds beautiful, like a church bell echoing out of the trees and the gardens full of flowers. Like he's awake.

TINY ZINNIAS

I RINSE my dark hairs from Tracie's orange razor in the tub. Fright and relief wash over me at once, like the steaming water I pour from a plastic cup over my back and chest and head. I get in here only three times a week since all of us share the full bath, so I soak awhile. Tonight I would like very much to lock the door, but it has no lock, so I do what Tracie does: put a chair outside in the hallway. She had me sit there and guard at first, till she trusted that when people saw the chair they'd leave her alone.

I feel the fright because I've shaved one strip of my leg, and my skin stings like it's on fire. I lather on more and more of Jude and Leonard's Gillette with aloe (Tracie can tell by smell that they use this aloe kind, and she said to use theirs and not the other that smells mean and piney like Morse—she keeps distance from Morse). So I smell like a shaving man and I feel like a firework.

But relief washes over, too, for tonight at supper she finally felt the baby move. We'd calculated the due date for December 2, once Nancy raised her nose from her charts and figuring—subtracting three months from the first day of Tracie's last menstruation, as best as Tracie could remember, and adding seven days; then checking it by counting ahead 266 days from the date of conception, as best as Tracie could remember. Tracie had squinched her eyes, smiled and looked dreamy. Unreliable, sighed Nancy, and she'd settled on December 2. That puts Tracie at five-and-a-half months here in the middle of August, so we've been looking at her belly, hoping every minute for a budge.

And tonight at the table, a budge. Tracie nearly tipped her water glass. Jude started crying. So it's alive then, I thought, and safe; it's true that it's able to breathe inside a sack of fluid; it hasn't drowned. After supper, I followed Tracie to our stoop and we felt for another small shove or wiggle, both our hands on her belly.

"You somersaulting thing," Tracie whispered. She wore her short stretchy skirt, and I found myself looking at her hairless legs. I wanted to touch them, but I touched my own instead. Thick with hair and coarse, the legs of a too-old little girl. She knew somehow.

"Once you start that, you can't stop," Tracie said. "Grows back pretty quick. A curse of being a woman." She rubbed up and down on her leg, and the smoothness didn't seem like a curse to me. I told her I'd be thirteen in less than two months—could I borrow her orange plastic razor that I'd seen on the tub's ledge?

It's like overgrown brush that the Division of Highway burns off from the ditch, my skin on fire underneath. I hold my breath and go for another swath. My blood has come again, after thirty-two days this time, two days late, but Nancy says that's still really regular. I've leaked some womb's blood into the bathwater, a drop like a little red fish. Now my cut leg hairs float in the water, too, and my leg is bleeding in places. I did not expect the razor to cut me. The cuts are tiny zinnias blooming till I wipe the blood away, but they bud and bloom and bleed again.

Another swath, and I feel deeper things, more secret than relief and fright, but still on the very surface of me, as if the very touchable outside is somehow my deepest part: I imagine Vaughn's hand on my leg now smooth, before I would push him away. And I imagine my own fingertips tracing the engraved letters on the fine memorial that's surely been delivered by now, with that angel standing by.

I had to wait a few days to steal from the purse, the tall wobbly box holding up that lamp. I had to wait till Jude cashed the check at the bank—he always gets cash and never deposits into a regular account since Leonard doesn't trust banks. Then I had to wait till I saw the stamped envelopes stacked on the table, which meant Jude had wrapped some of the cash in dark paper to pay the bills. Then I couldn't wait any longer. I didn't speak a word of it to Tracie. I don't know why for sure. Maybe I didn't want to worry her about having to steal her money back since she had a lot on her mind. Or maybe this was something I had to do alone.

I found Meadow View Memorials in the Yellow Pages and knew right away I'd order the grave marker pictured in their big ad. Their address was just outside of Dunlap. I dog-eared the page and hugged the Bell Atlantic book to my chest, watching Jude out the kitchen window. He was picking tomatoes and cucumbers for a salad because it said on the Xeroxes from Nancy, which he'd put up with magnets on the refrigerator, that a daily salad was good for Tracie's diet. I knew he'd take his time picking the best ripe tomatoes, so I snuck into his room and shut the door. I scanned the poems lining the shelf below the Bible commentaries and chose *A Memorial Collection of American Verse*. I chose it for the word *Memorial*, for the gold glittering on its spine, and for its size: it was thick enough that Jude wouldn't miss a page if I ripped it out. I flipped through with no idea what kind of poem goes on a headstone, but I saw the words "The Waking" and felt a shiver. I tore it fast and left a jagged edge and some of the words on the bottom of the poem, but it was only the first part I needed.

I went to bed wearing cutoffs and a tank top, covering up so Tracie wouldn't notice, though I was sweating underneath my bedspread. I waited till late, so late it was early, and I slipped downstairs into the Sanctuary, feeling my way without light. I moved the lamp, pulled up the knob on the loose lid, and took the wad of bills banded together in one bundle. Just like that. I put everything back in order, stuck the money in a paper sack, and crept back to bed in case Tracie would miss me. But I didn't sleep. I listened to the world not yet awake, to the sound of dreams, which I was afraid to bump or disturb or close a trapdoor on, but I knew I had to risk it. The horse hooves and the roll of the buggy came and went, with barely a pause. Then I finally heard Vaughn's car pull into the alley close to 5 a.m., and I bolted from bed.

Vaughn squinted at me where I stood bright in his headlights before he shut them off. The heat of the lights remained on me as I moved in the dark to the passenger door and opened it.

"Omi?" he said. "What the hell?"

I sat down on the low bench seat, its vinyl cool on my leg skin. For these summer months, I had confined myself to the house, then to the house and the garden barrels in back, then to the stoop watching the street with Tracie. I knew I could not go all the way, out past the edge of town, and buy the marker myself. I wasn't ready for that. So I had let my body move into Vaughn's long muscle car that smelled of cigarettes and seemed to drink me in like I was all liquid, all pool. I held the paper bag and the Yellow Pages in my lap. I shut the door.

I could make out the dark shape of a miniature dove hanging on a necklace chain from the rearview mirror, and that surprised me and kept me quiet. I felt his eyes and his close-by body. I felt my mistake then—how foolish this was—and I put my hand on the door handle.

"Easy, girl," said Vaughn to me.

I looked at him in the dark; he slumped and looked tired. Not seventeen years old, but older. Or maybe younger, sleepy and too boyish to have been pulling the heavy levers on heavy machines that bolted together those big vehicles. He unsnapped the front of his work shirt, slowly. Then he looked shy, I could tell even in the dark. Then he looked like something else, with heat in it, with danger.

"Don't go so quick," he whispered. "What's on your mind?"

I'd nearly forgotten what was on my mind because I felt a familiar vibration starting deep inside me. And I'd forgotten my shoes. I curled my toes hard into the dirty floor mat.

"Tracie's baby's twelve inches long," I blurted out, reaching for the first thing I could. "The book said that. And a pound and a half."

"Okay. That's what you came to tell me? At five in the morning?"

I covered my mouth, but only for a moment.

"Does she know whose kid it is?" he asked.

I pulled the door handle then, angry. "Of course she does."

"Hey, wait." Vaughn touched my knee without asking, then pulled away but not fast. "What's wrong with you? Sit here and talk to me."

I looked and he seemed to hold no teasing in his face, though I couldn't know for sure in the darkness.

"Sometimes you don't know," he said. "I've been looking at three different men my whole damn life, trying to see myself. Mom's never said, and I don't think she knows."

I let go of the handle and fingered the crinkly paper of the money bag in my lap.

"Will you do something for me?" I asked.

"What do you want?"

I opened to the dog-ear in the Yellow Pages and he switched on the dome light and leaned closer. I pointed to Meadow View's half-page ad, to the big black heart curved around by an angel's arms and wings, all on top of a flat slab of stone. There was carving you couldn't read inside the heart. Thirty-six inches tall and wide, it said underneath.

"Can you buy it, Vaughn? For Wood?"

He exhaled a long breath full of cigarette and coffee and metal.

I said, "You can get up to seventy-five letters and it can say whatever you want."

"That says three thousand dollars, Omi."

"No, it's on sale, see?" pointing to the corner. "Two thousand, four hundred."

"Fuck," he said in his wonder. "You crazy?"

I handed him my paper bag. "There's plenty."

"Fuck," he whispered again, handling the wad. "Where'd you get this?"

"Common Purse includes me, doesn't it?"

"And what happens when they miss the cash?"

"I wrote out here the words I want." I rush. "The ugly little marker that's there has his whole name on it. I just want Wood on this one. Here lies Wood. Born January 10, 1967, and died June 14, 1986." The Day of My Little Star, I thought. Vaughn was shaking his head and smoothing a loose end of black electrical tape on the steering wheel. From the back of the Yellow Pages I pulled the poem I'd torn from Jude's book. "I counted the letters, and you have enough for this, too. I just want the first line of it." I stuck in the poem to mark the Meadow View ad and set it on the black seat, though there was hardly room for it between us.

"It says top grade black stone," I said, "but could you order it blue or nice marble, if it's not too much trouble?" I was afraid he would ask why I was asking him, but he didn't ask, and I didn't know why.

"It'll probably be granite," he said. He put both arms across the top rim of the steering wheel and leaned forward, looking over at me. "You go out on the town with me. I'll get you this headstone if you go out on the town with me."

I said nothing, and he smiled and leaned back into the low seat so his chest skin—stretching over one rib bone then another—lay bare under the little light overhead. He turned his bleary eyes up to the light and switched it off. I felt his hand on my knee where he'd touched before. He laughed just a little, not a mean laugh, and not a sure one.

"You're growing up, you know. But you still have little girl legs."

I felt the vibration growing inside me, like when I'd lain on my bed looking at the ama divers that I would show my North. At the thought of North then, I felt a pang of sorrow and unfaithfulness and fear; I thought how I had been spending less time with him and more time with Tracie, studying up on pregnancy. Vaughn moved his hand up a little, off my bare skin onto the jean cutoffs covering my thigh. I sat still as a granite stone, holding my breath, wanting badly to know where his hand would go.

"Oh me, oh my," he whispered, and his voice shook me loose. I pushed his hand away, but not roughly.

"Tracie's going to miss me. She'll be up soon."

"I'll get the stone for you," he said.

"Thank you." And I was out of the muscle car without turning toward him again.

Tiny bits of toilet paper dot my shaved legs as I go looking for Tracie. All that day I was drowsy and nervous, not looking anyone in the eye. But a couple of weeks passed with no one noticing the missing cash, so I forgot about being nervous for a while; I thought more about Vaughn and his hand. She's still out on the stoop, but she must have gone inside to bring out her guidebook because it sits there on the lower step. Moths flit around the porch light.

"War wounds," she says, taking one look at me. She tries to laugh, but it sinks. "Wounds of women and girls." Something is wrong.

I sink, too, down on the steps beside her, to look for her in the place she's shifted to, out beyond the edge someplace. I want to finally tell her about the angel gravestone that could be there already—along the chain-link fence on the cemetery's steep slope—but since that wad of money was hers before she dropped it in, and since I took it without asking her first, I'm afraid to tell her the truth. I pick up the pregnancy book and open to her marker.

"Might not want to read that part," she says.

But it's too late. The black-and-white drawings are before me: a woman's legs spread and somebody's cut there; something sucking out the baby's head; huge pliers plucking another's head; and on the opposite page, a front view, the womb like a light bulb screwed into the pelvic bone and the baby sitting all wrong—the head's not down like a diver's—its legs are crossed, it's upright and they've drawn its face with tiny features of fear. "Breech," it reads underneath.

"The child can get strangled or suffocated," Tracie says. "And sometimes they slice you down there to get the head out, and stick all kinds of things up inside that you never thought could fit. I don't know if Miss Nancy got tools like that or not." Tracie's hands rub her belly that seems like it's grown bigger while I've been soaking in the bath. "Lots can go wrong with it. Complications. And it says here"—she points in the book—"there's more risk for teen girls." She squeezes her legs together a little then flips farther ahead. She points to a photo, not a drawing, of a woman looking dead and a bloody baby pulled right out of her sliced-up stomach; its face looks up into some light like a car's dome light in the darkness. "Sometimes," she says, "they have to cut the baby out in a C-section."

"You afraid?" I whisper. I shiver and look away from the photo. She doesn't answer for a while and a car speeds by, throwing headlights across her nervous face.

"I wish I wasn't doing this alone," she says. "I wish he was here."

And I know she means the man who loved her and left.

"I'm here," I say, and I plan to be there on December 2. "You feel it move again?"

"No. Maybe that one flip wore her out." Tracie finds her laugh, though it's thin, and the sad curve is deep in her shoulders underneath her hot sweater. "You got to get you some lotion on them legs, Omi Ruth. Come on"—she stands—"before prayer circle at nine."

Upstairs, we hear somebody showering in the full bath, but I know where North's lotions and salves are, the ones Jayne brings for him and stows under his bed. We rub them on his feet for circulation and on his hands so dry like tissue paper. There's one that smells like new leaves, and I tell Tracie we can put that on my legs. She follows me into North's room farther than she has before; usually she stays at the doorway like she's shy.

"It's me," I say to him and slide out the tray of lotions on the floor. I choose the bottle I want and squirt it and spread it up and down. Each bit of toilet paper hurts a little to take off and lets a little bloom of blood surface again, but not much.

"What's that smell?" Tracie asks.

I sniff but don't smell anything besides the tree-leaf lotion I smear.

"It's ointment," she says, "like the camphor Mama'd put on bug bites."

And I smell it then. "I'm just used to it, I guess. We put his Bag Balm on today. For his bedsores." The square green tin of salve sits on the lotion tray, too, and I hold it out to show her.

"That's for a cow's udder," says Tracie to me, and I'm embarrassed for him, though she's right; it says so right on the lid and has a picture of a cow.

"Jayne says the hospitals use it," I say, "not just the farm vets," but Tracie studies the pink teats on the lid. I'm hurt at first, till I see she means no harm to him. I see that her fear is still lurking around, her fear of a blade's slit on her secret skin, or of her baby strangling inside her. Maybe she's the opposite of me, and North's place between living and dying only makes her more afraid instead of less. I see him for a moment as she sees him: skin and bones and tubes and the soft brown spots of age. I have to close my eyes to see his light coming through again, and it comes. "Isn't it horrible," she asked me once, "caring for him?" "No," I told her, but I didn't say why and I wasn't sure that I could.

"Let's fold up these towels," I say like Jayne, trying to soothe Tracie's fear with chores. I'm Jayne's Ruthie, and Tracie folds one towel then another, taking them from the chair back.

"I just need a distraction," she says. "It's too quiet here. I can't even watch soaps on TV."

Jayne has made a shelf in the closet out of cardboard boxes, and I put our stack of towels in there. I look down and think about the cubby full of stolen things from Wood's room. I've not moved them since the day of his burial.

"I have an idea," I say, and I grope around in the cubby till I find the tape and his radio that tunes in and records and plays back.

TODAY I AM ASMA

AT THE prayer circle I fidget next to Tracie, nervous about the wooden box under that lamp, the Common Purse that's short a couple thousand, but nobody looks at it, so I focus on sitting carefully with the tape and radio in my two back pockets; then it's my game with the shoes. It's Tracie's old black boots I start with, counting their twelve pairs of holes for laces in my mind's eye, peeking to see that I'm right.

Leonard is so longwinded tonight, I have to reach for other people's feet, people who are not in this room with paisley carpet: Reagan's bright white shoes, with the rounded Nike checkmark in dark blue, how they match exactly the ones Spencer wore into the kitchen that day to deliver the sack of radishes he wished were flowers. Boys in new shoes and my own bare feet on a floor mat, sandy and torn at the corner, in Vaughn's muscle car, and my not seeing his feet beside the clutch and pedals down in the darkness, but I know they're steel toes like Morse's, and I know Vaughn's hand on my lotioned leg would be strong enough to take me to someplace out on the town, a place far outside this one. I start to feel hot on my neck, so I quit that picture.

I pat my back pocket and listen for the way Wood's voice will sound on the tape's radio show. I can't quite hear it because lately his funny voices have faded for me, just like his face, though never his laugh. I'm listening for his laugh when the amens murmur into the tin can on the string.

Tracie and I slip upstairs and sit under our Big Top till we think we've heard all the footsteps we need to. She changes into Sue's lavender robe in the bathroom then we sneak back down, into Wood's empty room, and shut the door. I don't want to turn on the light and risk being discovered, so we sit on the cool bare mattress waiting for our eyes to get used to the dark. Then, on the windowsill, I see a candle. There are matches so I light it, like this is some kind of ceremony. The candle wax is burnt down a little. Somebody's been in here.

"Must be Carson," I whisper and look at Tracie, but she's lying back on the bed already, her knee folded up into the air and her hand on her naked belly, feeling for that second somersault. She's wearing pretty black panties trimmed in lace.

"So I want to play you a tape," I say. "A real good distraction." And I sit beside her on the bed and tell her how things were with Wood and me, making radio shows. I'm sturdy as I talk—I don't waver—because I'm doing this for her. I tell her how we started because of Leonard's awful sermons that he tapes and mails in to Christian radio, always with a pitch for donations at the end, but no money ever comes in. Wood hated the thought of Leonard's voice broadcasting into people's homes in Dunlap, even homes over in South Bend since the signal could stretch that far. Wood said radio needed voices that talked right to you, like you weren't a stranger. He said radio should make people feel less alone.

He wanted to do his own show, but with what machine? He had to get Leonard to buy him a radio that could record, so Wood said he wanted to follow in our law-father's footsteps and needed to practice. It wasn't true, but it got him his radio. And we pretended it was true so he wouldn't get caught. We'd make the tapes on Sundays and talk the first part of the tape just like Leonard's sermon, so that if anybody played it back, they'd see we were sincere. We made the tape covers look like missionary shows for kids out there; Wood wrote on the tape jacket the name of some city of the world he was preaching to.

I hold up the stolen tape for Tracie. "See how this says 'Tehran'? I don't know where that is, but that was where we were missionaries for this one, or said we were. Wood knew all the countries—that's his handwriting. And he wrote down the date we made it, Easter 1983, so I was only a child, nine years old, and he was sixteen, like you." I am more and more of a chatty-box because Tracie has slipped away again, to that place out along the edge. I need to get her back, to distract her from sadness and fear. She just looks up at the ceiling, at the candle's flickering hoop of light. I go on.

"My job was to cut out a child-face from *The Macedonian Call*, like we were praying for that child to be saved by Jesus—you could tell I'd be a girl to make collage later on. See this?" I open the plastic tape cover to take out the picture folded inside. A face with four fold creases looks out at me. "Asma," it reads under the photo in my childish print, the little *a* made backward like I used to do, with the stem on the left side. "Asma," I say. "That must have been her name in *The Call* article." I touch this girl's face, at the tip-top of her cheekbone. "I remember her," I whisper. Then I go quiet.

Tracie hasn't looked over; she stays out there on the edge and I let her. Asma is covered in a white veil, over her head like the Amish girls, smooth and tucked, but on her face, too—white lace over her nose and below, like a pretty scarf on a thief. Her deep brown forehead shows, and the storm-cloud edge of her black hair pulled back. Then it's just her eyes, and the dark crescent moons of eyebrows, charcoal moons, and her lashes so long. I remember finding her face among all the others on all the pages because hers was the most beautiful. And the last time our eyes met, I was a child. Now what am I? Her eyes are pearls blacker than Tracie's. Her eyes are the same forever. I wonder, are mine? My eyes that are Wood's?

"So we told everybody it was a mission radio show for kids." I mumble now, not supposing Tracie is with me at all. "And we'd start it out that way. Then, after a while, we'd say whatever we wanted—do commercials and voices, make fun of the C.P. people, do jokes, and he took song requests, like it was call-in. Wood was never shy on tape like he was in real life." I lay Asma on the bed with care and slip the tape into the radio's slot. It's not rewound all the way, but almost, and I don't rewind it. "We'll have to listen quietly because of Loomis there"—I'm pointing to the wall. I lie down beside a faraway Tracie Casteel and pull Asma up close to me, holding her face so that her white veil is touching this old tank top of Lucy's. I push *play*.

. . . *and make it out of gopherwood. Make rooms in the ark and cover it inside and out with pitch. And later on, God says he will bring a flood on the earth, to destroy from under heaven all flesh in which is the breath of life. But God said to Noah, I will establish my covenant with you. So Noah and his law-sons and their law-wives got in the ark and brought with them two of every animal to save them. Naomi Ruth, tell the kids all the things God protected on the ark.—Two puppies! Two zebras and chipmunks! And tigers!—That's right, and into the ark they went, and then the rain started to pour.*

I push *stop*. I let go of the breath I didn't know I was holding. "That's me," I whisper. "I sound like a baby." Here I am with Wood. He sounds like he's inside a cave. I go in to search for him. "I'll fast-forward," I say. "This is the pretend part to fool Leonard, the Bible story and the faithfulness that gets the rainbow. It was Easter that day—I remember Jude helping us make kites out of newsprint, and mine had Noah's rainbow on it. This will be the real part." I stop the speedy reels to push *play* again.

"Tracie? You listening?"

"Mmhmm?"

. . . the man puts his booger in a little coin purse in his suit pocket, and the boys ask him, "What're you doing there, sir?" "Boys, I'm saving that for later!" the man says. "Waste not want not."—Eeeyew, Wood!—Waste not, want not. Now don't turn your dial, folks at home, you're listening to the Omi-Wood Show, right here on 90.3 FM! It's a hot one today, 78 degrees and rising—

His clowning voice goes muffled, laughing.

Quit covering my mouth!—You quit being so gross!—Okay, okay. You still taping, Omi? Check it. Okay. Now here, okay, here we are. Look here at what I have. Let's see, I put it right under . . . Taa-dah!— You saved it!—Of course I saved it. Listeners out there, I have in my hand a keychain given to me by none other than my little sister in the studio with me here today. Say hi there, Omi Ruth.—Hi there, folks at home.—And tell them just where you got this fine keychain.—You know where I got it.—Omi, for the listeners at home.

My giggling voice goes loud, the mic up close to my mouth, his funny magician voice in the background, like you'd hear under a carnival tent.

I got it at the flea market stand when Sue took me. My favorite one with the T-shirts and license-plate magnets that say your name. And you can get things airbrushed on.—And tell our listeners how's come you purchased this fine item?—I got it for you last Easter for driving with Morse when he teaches you. And you saved it!—Folks, you should see the quality and the workmanship of this deluxe keychain. Gold hubcaps on a little Corvette, the body's red with white seats and a tiny handsome driver who looks, well, he looks just like your own host here over the airwaves. The key ring hooks right into the rearview mirror, ready for my set of keys.

It's a deep salesman voice and something even smoother, ducking and dipping low, me giggling again, goofy and too close to the mic.

Of course I saved it. And, folks, I myself have a gift for none other than Omi Ruth this Easter.—You do? Wood, you do?—I have a gift she'll get tonight after supper as long as she's my servant all day and brings me anything I want.—Wood!—I could go for a bottle of Coke please—Wood!—and a burger, no mayonnaise—Quit! What is it? What did you get me?—maybe a chocolate shake, no, hold the shake because it's time for the call-in portion of our show—Wood!—and, callers, today we'd like to hear from you, about things you've saved over time. That charm your sweetheart slipped you in the moonlight— those fancy shoes you danced in down a glossy gym floor—and maybe that prize trophy from the best game of the season.

Crooning like he's heard the real radio men do, as if he's planting sweet memories in your head.

Deep in your chest of drawers and under your bed, find your most prized possessions. And send them on into the station. We'll put all these fine things . . .

Footsteps go away then come back.

I smile about the beat-up box he found in the closet. I remember he did not give me an Easter gift.

. . . right in here, in this time capsule.—That's a shoebox, Wood.— No, no, not just any old shoebox. This is a box we'll bury in the ground full of all the things the people of Dunlap have saved. That's right, so call in at 444-WAJR, that's 444-WAJR, and tell us on the air about the special gifts you've tucked away. What would you like to show people one hundred years in the future when they dig up this time capsule?—Shoebox from the dollar store.—Time capsule, folks—

Carson's voice calling from far away, through the door, calling in to the radio show. *Woodrun, Omi, come out for lunch*, she says.

Just whispers now:

Things you save. Come on.—Smooth river rocks.—And we have a caller already, Omi Ruth herself.—And Lucy's Care Bear that's like new.—I have this keychain and a pair of headphones from Jude.— Pictures.—Postcards.—The tiny monkey statue that came in the Red Rose tea box.—That's a good one.—And the last piece of a pack of Doublemint, I save it forever—

Carson's voice louder and closer this time: *Now, you two. Put it away.*

Then a loud thick thump that means the *stop* button pushed down to end the recording, and then silence without the story of the time capsule. But the tape plays on, just the soft *chirr* of the little reels still making friction. I'm furious at Carson, interrupting this only radio show I have. She is Farmer Booth in the hayfield keeping me from Wood's things with wings, Booth saying, "A boy got cut up behind the tractor one time and no one swooped in to save him from it."

Is Tracie at all close to me lying here? I feel Asma along the creases of her photo. I've followed Wood's silly voice into the cave of played-back sound, his voice that's a glow-in-the-dark snake. His voice that goes three ways at least, not in layers like Leonard's, but in a star with legs going out and out—it goes teasing and gentle, goes like dynamite about to blow, and like sweet creek-water cooling, pooling, moving on. It's creek-water down my cheeks. The first real tears I've shed since he died. I feel Tracie's hand take mine. She's come back to me.

Another loud thump surprises us after the silence. A thump that means he recorded again. It's all whisper so we lean in.

Today was Easter. I got Naomi the perfect gift, a little peep from the hardware store. We walked there with Vaughn last week to get the rods for the kites. Vaughn and me had the dowels cut and she just stood at the cage and watched all the baby chicks huddle together. She couldn't have been happier. They're just two days old, the clerk said. Omi petted them through the cage and woke them up. They cried loud, in one big chirp, and I could tell the clerk was annoyed. I asked him how to take care of it and how much it would be. I went by myself to get her one later. It was a yellow fluff ball with hardly any body when you picked it up.

A pause of quiet. But reels were still collecting sound, like they were greedy, as greedy as me. For I don't remember this part of the show, and I understand that I was nowhere near the mic. He whispers alone. It's Wood and the radio with no Omi, and plain, with no funny voices. This leg of his voice-star is just a boy at sixteen keeping secrets from me. What baby chick? I remember the cage at the hardware store, but I never held one of my own.

I took it home and did what he said. I hooked up a lamp over a box to keep it warm. Jude let me keep it in his room. I put feed in a lid, like he said, and a bowl for water. I shouldn't have done that, or not such a big one, I guess. Maybe it was too young. I think it needed to curl up with the rest of them and hide in all their feathers to stay alive. I checked on it all the time. It quit walking around and just slept by the feed. It didn't eat. I picked it up and held it on Easter and it shook inside its tiny chest. It felt like its heart was beating too hard and it was about to shrivel up, and I put it right beside the water bowl so it would drink. We did our radio show and ate a ham lunch and when I came back, it had drowned in the bowl. It was floating there. I tried to save it but I could tell its heart wasn't beating. I took it behind the house and dug a hole to bury it.

Quiet again, but the reels and the reels. Then a sniff like he's crying.

It's Tracie who pushes *stop*.

I remember he didn't fly kites with me in the park. My rainbow kite alone in the sky. I didn't know. He never told me, till this tape. I'll save this tape till it melts in the center of the earth or wears out, but I won't let it wear out. I'll only play it sometimes.

I look over and Tracie's face is wet.

"My baby moved again," she says. "She did a flip."

"I never knew that part," I say. I'm crying but not as hard as I want to, for these tears have been a long time coming. I unclasp hands with her and touch her belly. I hold Asma in the other hand, Asma who knew about the little peep; she was there when he recorded. "He had a whole box. A million tapes, and this is the only one I could grab before they sold them or threw them out. Maybe he taped lots of beautiful secrets on there without me. How could I not know things?"

"People are deep wells of water," says Tracie to me. Her eyes are closed and I close mine, thinking we'll see his starry voice still hanging in the air. "There's so much inside. And we never touch bottom."

"Then he's a stranger to me," I weep out.

"No, he ain't a stranger." And she rubs her belly over the child who twists and turns in that place between living and dying. My North, I wonder then—can he see the baby there?

I hold Asma to catch the candlelight and I know why she is so beautiful to me: because she is so secret. Are her legs hairless, are her teeth crooked, do her curls coil into knots under her veil? What language is on her lips I can't see? I let her go, I let Tracie go, and I sit up and wrap my hair, long as Carson's, around my face. I wrap and wrap my hair, my veil.

Today I am Asma.

I am just these eyes. I am beautiful and not good. For I have secrets, too.

I lie back with my veil wrapped around. Tracie and me, we lie there on Wood's bare bed till the candle burns out and we see only what that drowned baby chick could see.

I finally tell her in the darkness.

"I have bought a grave marker for Wood. Vaughn's done it for me. I spent all your government check, I stole it from the purse, and there's an angel."

Silence and her knee slips down, both legs straight. "Have you gone to see it?"

"No. Not yet."

"Then come on, Omi Ruth."

We are back in our Big Top closet-room, and it's so late into the night, it's almost morning. Tracie moves fast, digging in her duffle bag in the corner. She pulls out clothes I've not seen before, then a plastic pouch from the front pocket where she kept the Coal Lick postcard before she gave it to me.

"Put this on," she says, handing me a dress. It's blue with white polka dots and a thin white belt, capped sleeves and a low back. She disappears before I can speak; I hear her in the full bath. She comes back wearing a yellow dress that I can tell is too tight for her belly, a white sweater buttoned overtop; her silver hoops still swing from her changing so fast.

"I don't wear black to a funeral," she says. "And neither do you."

I think, What funeral?

She takes hold of my tank top at the bottom and pulls it off, right over my head, so I'm naked above the waist. I cover my chest.

"Don't now, don't cover yourself. You ain't got no idea how pretty you are."

I'm stunned as she pulls the polka-dotted dress down over my head and bends my arms through, like I'm made of rubber. *Pretty.* The dress is big enough to contain me and cover me, not too small like Lucy's things. It's even a bit loose at the waist till she buckles the belt.

Then she unzips the plastic pouch and takes out a small mirror and a tube of lipstick. She holds the mirror to her mouth, spreading the bright red on her lips, so expert, her mouth in a skinny *O*. I've never seen her wear lipstick before.

"Come on," she says, about to put it on my lips, but I pull back.

"I don't want it," I say. "Wood said it makes me look dumb." I think she looks prettier than all the women in Lucy's fashion catalogs.

"He really said that?"

"No, I just know."

"Listen, Omi. He just didn't want to see his baby sister grow up." She touched the red tip to my top lip first. I make the skinny *O*. "Now rub together like this." She holds the mirror to my lips. "You like it?"

I nod, yes, I do. Very much.

"Okay then." Tracie rummages deeper into her duffle and pulls out one red shoe then another. "These'll match your lips. But carry them till we get outside."

"Tracie, where?"

"We're gonna go see that grave marker."

"How?" I whisper. "It's all the way across town."

"We'll take Morse's truck." She grins and carries her boots that have carried her all over this world.

We tiptoe downstairs and into the kitchen, open the cabinet door where Morse keeps the keys, but they're not there.

"Shit," she says.

"Shit," I echo through my red lips. We stand still, thinking, how to get there?

"All dressed up and no place to go," she says, sadder than I can take.

Then I hear it: hooves on pavement, rolling wooden wheels.

"Come on," I say, taking her hand and pulling fast. I swing open the back door and smack right into Spencer Frye, so hard he nearly drops the eggs. I'm up close, on top of his black T-shirt smelling earthy, his eyes as wide as Tracie's. He doesn't speak but I still say, "Shh." I keep hold of her hand to help her into the black buggy in the alley; I climb in beside her and leave the door open, leaving him space on the thin bench. And here he comes, without a word, shutting the door and *nick nicking* the horse with the gentlest tug of the reins. Too dark to see much, but I know it's his jeans here beside my white polka dots on blue. We pull forward and I realize I didn't ever tell my North good-night.

All around our feet, dozens and dozens of eggs. Good thing we still hold our shoes in our hands, now in our laps. We all three look out the front square windows with no glass, wind playing with our curls. It's all black inside here, a little scary. Tyrone Road, the horse tail, the porch lights passing—it's all framed in black by the square windows. This is the way he sees the waking-up world. We're at the end of Tyrone, and I hear Vaughn's car take the corner, not that far away, back at the other end.

My pretty red mouth speaks: "Tracie Casteel, this is Spencer Frye."

"Hi there," says Tracie, as if riding in a horse and buggy is something she does every day, as if we're going to the grocery store in a taxi, as if this isn't my very first time away from Solomon's Porch in two months. This is the shy boy with the radishes, I think to her, and before that, the jars full of flowers. He will take us wherever we want; I know I'm right.

"Naomi?" Spencer asks, like he's not sure it's me. His hair is even longer now, so his face is in full shadow, behind the curtain of his bangs. I'm in a party dress fit to mourn in, and I put my hand on his that holds the reins. I slip my fingers right into the spaces between his; his hand's all butter. I think how it's the other way around from me and Vaughn—Vaughn whose hand touched my knee and did all the work.

"Where would you like to go?" Spencer asks, formal as a chauffeur.

Then we're not on Tyrone anymore. We're through the traffic light, by Chalkers pool hall with all its beer signs dark; we're on Jackson, we're on Fifth. "Well," I say. We're under streetlamps; the Kroger glows its tired twenty-four-hour glow. "Well." Two months since I've seen the world beyond our stoop.

"We need to visit the cemetery," says Tracie, seeing my tongue won't work. And Spencer nods as if it's every day he carries to the graveyard two hitchhikers wearing lipstick and holding their shoes, one holding his hand.

"It's Ace Hardware," I say, pointing like a child to the chain store, same as the one back on Tyrone, but I don't feel like a child; I feel too full of memory. A cage of chicks probably in there, and one of them, a cold sickly one, for me. I grip Spencer's hand harder now and he moves the reins to his other, turning us onto Main that will take us across town. Shadowy men appear under the lamps, disappear and appear again in the next circle of light; lunch buckets, work shirts like Vaughn's, going on shift. The world of Dunlap is going on shift every day of its life, and today I am seeing it. It's nearly dawn.

"So, you're an Amish?" says Tracie.

"Yes," he says. "I am a Frye, raised in the Old Order."

"You don't dress too Amish."

Spencer tosses his hair to the side and looks over at us for the first time. He doesn't explain his rumspringa to her, and I wonder if maybe he's already chosen the world and turned his back on his people. This world with warehouses stretching out, opening a heavy-eyelid door to a tractor-trailer at the loading dock. And the used RV outlet with a "Big Sale Now," RVs bolted together decades ago by the kinds of levers Vaughn and Morse pull down, RVs hauled out across the highways, just to be sold here, with a new air conditioner installed. Spencer and me, have we chosen all this?

"I see you are having a child."

"Baby girl, yessir. I'm that big, mmhmm? Well, it's good she's growing. She did some somersaults last night." She rubs. "What about your eggs?"

"Later will be fine."

I see Cindy Lane's, windows cheery with light through blue curtains. Up beyond it, far past the edge of town, the radio tower you hardly see unless it's dark out, its blinking red light. Spencer nods toward the diner. "I will need to start work at 8:30. Is it your brother, Naomi? Is it his grave?"

"Yes." I close my eyes, suddenly wanting to sleep. We haven't slept all night. I lay my head on Spencer Frye's shoulder and hear Tracie humming quietly, some gospel song I don't know.

It's nearly light enough to see the headstones, and we make our way toward the steep slope at the graveyard's edge. The climb is not easy for Tracie, though her black boots help keep her steady. I'm wearing red shoes I could dance in. Spencer said he'd wait for us by the road.

White stone crosses and gray rainbow arcs and diamond shapes. Moss covering one stone like a shawl. A tiny American flag stuck in the ground, and a cluster of silk flowers. Another. The glow beyond the steep slope is the Wendy's parking lot.

Thirty-six inches by thirty-six. I try to match that to a stone, but I've only seen the small picture in the ad. I don't see it anywhere. I get to the top just before Tracie, and none of the stones are right. A fear strikes me: hoodlum. She said that about Vaughn and Odell. He's stolen the money. No, no, no. Please no. I spin around, angry, but then I see her over on the ground, squatting in her tight yellow dress. She has found it.

It is just as fine as I've imagined.

It's not blue—it's granite like Vaughn said—but I don't mind. I am sorry, Vaughn Buey, that I thought you'd steal from me. The angel's left arm stretches all the way over the heart, the other arm hugging the side. I don't see the little ugly stone with only his name, so they must have put it exactly on top.

"In Loving Memory" carved at the heart's crest; that must have been thrown in for free since I used up the seventy-five letters. "Here lies Wood," just like I wanted it, and the dates just right. I read the line of the poem out loud: "I wake to sleep, and take my waking slow." It is perfect, it is a mystery like prayer, it is engraved in cursive that moves like waves of water.

"I've never seen one this pretty," says Tracie to me from her squat on the ground. Her fingers play on the angel's cheek that leans onto its top outstretched arm, like mine, so easy, on Spencer's shoulder.

You're in shabby corduroys, I think to Wood, but with the fanciest of stones. His soul fluttering in me. It flutters till I look down into the graveyard and see a shape there. A woman. She is alone, pitched forward over a plainer stone than this, one rounded on top. She almost touches it with her forehead, she's bending so low. I feel like I know her. Maybe I do. You are alone but not alone, I think to her from inside my hermit-crab shell. For here we are too—and something opens in me, a little door that I look through. A picture forms, like collage, and my face is next to other faces, like this bent woman's, and Asma's, and the faces of those men heading to work, and faces that surprise me, like Reagan's face next door and his sisters' faces I've never seen, and the girl's face who lost her leg on the train tracks in Detroit. I see North then, I see him and Loomis when Loomis wore lipstick and their hands clasped like a bracelet. I think: I am somehow here for them too, though aren't they still living and not buried? A bunch of faces like flowers, and I am there among so many others in Spencer's jar. It's a pretty thought. I see it all only for a moment, then the small door closes and it fades into what Tracie is saying, into the curve of the angel's body she strokes.

"You can say anything you want," she whispers to me, "cause I know Leonard's voice was the only one at the funeral you had, mmhmm? That right?"

"That's right." It was Leonard's voice that day, and the lousy hymn-singing and Lucy hissing at her girls to be still.

"We can say whatever we want, Omi."

Then I know Tracie could somehow see my vision too—just

now—and I know that we are here to mourn big, to mourn in the wide sunrise-arc Nancy Calhoun makes like a fool with her arms, to mourn the sunrise itself. So I start. "I would've named the baby chick Marigold. I think it would have been yellow and poofy like that."

Tracie's turn. "We got a letter from my Aunt Gail. That's how we knew Daddy's lungs had given out. He was in Baltimore fixing up mowers and motorbikes."

"My brother Wood was nineteen and a car hit head-on."

"Mama drank herself to death. Poisoned her liver and kept it from me till she couldn't anymore."

"Wood grew up and had a secret I never knew."

"He'd have shared it with you when it was time."

"I know."

"You made them collages for him. And the wall in the back with the broken blue dishes."

"Yes. And you're lonely here. In Coal Lick the houses make a ring, and you miss it."

"You don't have to be so afraid to leave the house."

"Your baby's coming. She is safe and sound."

We're both in the grass's dew, party dresses damp. Holding each other for a long time, till we hear some cars in the Wendy's parking lot beyond, and I think Spencer has waited long enough.

Along the chain-link fence, black-eyed Susans shoot up in bright bunches. We brush away the trash, a crushed cup that a Frosty came in, spoons and wrappers. We pull up a few of the black-eyed Susans; we have to pull hard since their roots are deep.

A bouquet of yellow flowers at the angel's feet, and we're

making our way back to the buggy at the road, so tired and emptied out.

Spencer Frye gets the horse going at a good pace to get us back. It must be close to 8:30 a.m., close to when he needs to be at work, and there are the eggs to deliver, too. We get down from the buggy in the alley, and he helps us, like we're real ladies. Chastity Buey is there on her back steps smoking a cigarette in her striped waitress clothes.

"You girls look like you've been to church," she says to us. "Or a big dance someplace."

We're so soft and weary, we just smile.

"Is that where you've taken them, Spencer? To church?" She knows him from the diner, I remember. Her voice is sweet, smooth like Vaughn's. She has lipstick on that's a shade lighter than mine.

"Yes, I took them to church with me," Spencer lies. It's not even Sunday.

"Well, I bet you all were a sight to see on an Amish church bench." She puts out her cigarette on the stone step and laughs. "Don't worry," she whispers, "I won't tell."

I help Tracie to the door and look back at Spencer without having words to thank him. He touches my back briefly where the dress shows my skin. Tracie and me are inside when I hear Chastity ask for a ride into work so she won't have to take the bus. Another woman wearing lipstick and stepping gingerly around his dozens of undelivered eggs.

Nobody's in the kitchen, which is a relief, and Tracie sneaks upstairs. I follow but not before I slip into Wood's room and collect the radio, the tape, and Asma's creased face.

Upstairs, I turn the old crystal knob and find Jayne and Regina changing his sheets. I rub my sleepy eyes, setting the radio on the floor in the doorway and switching it on. Tuning through static till I get a pop song that Regina doesn't seem to hear, but Jayne hears and turns toward me.

"Well, now. Just look at you. You're looking so pretty."

I stay in the doorway, leaning my weight into the frame but feeling light.

"Turn that on up, Ruthie," says Jayne to me, gently weaving her big body in a sway. She pulls his curtains open. "He won't mind that music one bit."

ENTERTAINING ANGELS

IT'S BEEN a week since our private funeral and still not a word about the missing money. So I try to forget about it. I go looking for Nancy's pillow kit under my bed. While I'm there, I dust off the collages I've outgrown and my stack of magazines—ama divers on top—and I look for a moment at my soft postcard from Coal Lick where there are more trees than houses so the cabins hug together for comfort. Maybe Tracie will take me there one day, me and her newborn. I tuck the postcard back under the bed and carry the pillow kit in its cellophane over to North's room. I have a little interest in sewing, now that Nancy's backed off on it and everything that comes out of her mouth concerns birthing babies.

It's late afternoon, after Jayne's bathed North, and it's my shift to sit by him and turn him every so often till Regina comes with new medicine and food packs for the IVs. I'm to turn him one way then another—for the bedsores have gotten worse— and moisten his mouth with the sponge. I spread the kit onto the floor—"Oversized Envelope Pillow Slip." Nancy wants to throw a baby shower, so I need a gift to give. In the picture on the booklet of directions, the big pillow sits on a big gold sofa like nothing in Solomon's Porch. It says I need fiberfill to stuff it with, but that's not included in the kit. Well, I think, it looks to me like I can use this pattern a few times over and stretch the slip into a quilt, or a blanket that's baby size. And this baby's coming in December so she'll need a warm blanket, though on a day like today I can't imagine feeling chill. One hundred and three, it said on the thermometer at noon, hottest day on record this summer. Everything in the garden barrels is wilting; the air's so thick with drops of water we can't see, we've put all the window fans on high, trying to suck in the relieving storm they say is on the way.

There's a white polyester-cotton blend for the backing and all the rest are wild fabrics in three types of blue: a deep midnight with swirls kind of like the paisleys in the Sanctuary carpet, but more like comets in outer space; turquoise swimming with yellow and green fish; and an ice-blue like Spencer's eyes and Jude's, rippled through with sound waves. But blue is for a boy, so I need to add something for her baby girl, since we just know it's a girl. I go to the cardboard-box shelves in the closet, and, yes, there's that pink towel of North's that's got a hole at the edge; the nurses won't miss it. And I can see into the cubby, Wood's stolen pair of red shorts. I can use red. I leave the blue denim jacket, but grab his undershirt for more white.

I wait for the fierce flutter in my chest, but nothing comes, so I don't think Wood will mind being part of the baby blanket. You rest better now, don't you, I think to him. Something is looser in me, too, my limbs and hair and feet; I'm freer in motion. And maybe even Tracie's curve of sadness is easing. Just knowing that angel marker is there, I catch myself smiling. I can almost forget that the Common Purse will soon be found empty and someone will have to give an account.

At least that day is not today.

I'm cheery as I rise from the floor to tend my North. I go first to the far window to see whether Vaughn's black shade is raised. It is, and I hope hard to see his chest, his arms, but he must be gone. I touch my thigh where he touched me, in his low muscle car. Then I turn to the other window, and I reach to the sill for the sponge for North's lips when I find his eyes open and looking straight at me.

Oh my.

I drop the sponge onto his chest, a bloom of wet on his nightshirt.

"North," I whisper. "North?" like I'm not sure it's him, he looks so strange with these gray-green eyes, the pupils so huge in the middle but shrinking fast to pinheads. I pull back his curtains; I raise the half-up window all the way, begging for a breeze for him who is awake.

Awake.

"North, can you talk to me? It's me, it's Omi Ruth. Can you say hello?" Oh but what beautiful girl has he seen with his fingertips? Could it be the same girl he looks at now? I take his hand. Smaller and darker go the center pupils. I am a grown woman and a tiny child, both at once. I thrill and I choke. "Can you tell me what you see?"

And in comes Regina through the door. I throw my eyes at her, wishing she were Jayne. "He's awake!" I say. "Look!"

She does not come running. She walks evenly to me in her ugly, solemn navy blouse, already with her latex gloves on. She takes the little sponge from its water-blossom on his chest and puts it back in the bowl on the sill.

"Don't you see?" I'm mad at her preciseness and at the IV pouches she holds, like they will only put him back to sleep, send him back, so I knock them from her hands to the floor.

"Naomi!" she yells and grabs my arm.

"No!" and I fight, I skirt around her and step on a busted bag and on my ripple-blue fabric, which makes me madder, but she doesn't let go. She surprises me: she pulls me right into her thin flat chest and holds me there, won't let me budge when I try to push free.

"Stop," she says, calm. "Just stop this."

I go limp, but only because I plan to shock her and break free, but it's like she knows that and holds me more and more tightly. So tightly, her heartbeat is a thunder inside me.

"Listen to me, girl." She's never spoken so softly, not Regina. "You have to let him go. Look at his eyes." She keeps hold, but turns me to see his wakeful eyes. They don't look at me; they look up where they looked before. "He can't hear or think or see. It's just his muscles. His body has automatic behaviors that don't require the thinking part of the brain. He's in a vegetative state, Naomi. Most people don't last more than four weeks. My longest living patient lasted six months to the very day of her admission to hospice. I don't wish that for anybody."

"He's awake," I whisper, stubborn.

"He's not. He's gone over two months like this and I hope not much longer. This man needs to go."

"He *is* awake! How else could he be hearing all the way up to the end?"

"You can't listen to Jayne, Naomi. She means well, but she's not telling the truth."

I look at his eyes staring straight up. At nothing? "He's in between living and dying," I say.

"That could be. But you can't stay there too long."

I want to say, "You're mean, Regina, you're bitter and mean." But I don't say a word and she does not stop holding me. She rocks me a little in her strong, exact arms.

"You need to let him go." She says it more gently than I thought she could speak.

Jayne sweeps into the room right then, in her teddy-bear pullover dripping with sweat, with a cool rag twisted around her big neck. "Oh, honey. What is it, my Ruthie?"

I break from Regina and bury my face into the wet teddy bears, into her pillowy chest. "I thought he woke up," I say. I felt free before, planning my sewing project, knowing Wood was pleased. But now these eyes have opened and they see without seeing and ask to be let go. I feel what he feels, I feel the aloneness of this house. Each of us in a faraway corner. Deeper into Jayne's chest and I hear her heartbeat as thunder, too, till I realize the thunder is real. It's outside. The storm has come.

And it is no timid sprinkle, how the Indiana rain usually starts, with a clatter on the gutters and the small tin roof over the stoop. No, it comes in a *burst*, in a sheet, and it comes with wind. I have just raised his window, so a gust of rain washes in and drenches him, just like that, like God pouring a bucket down. Surely North will jump and shake himself off, but no, he lies more still than ever. Regina quickly pulls the window down. All the blue fabrics on the floor turn a deeper, wetter blue, like we're standing in ocean. I picture his pupils dissolving in the rain like black salt. Leaving only the gray-green, hard pretty gems.

"Help!" Tracie yells from over in our Big Top. "Omi Ruth! Help me, it's stuck!"

I let loose of Jayne and run to my room where Tracie is

soaked to the bone in a whirlwind of rainwater, the box fan still on high with a mind of its own. She holds up her hands in a useless umbrella, laughing; she holds the fan's knob in her hand.

"It's stuck!" she yells, though I'm right beside her in the downpour. "I tried to shut it down but the switch came off!"

I think fast, I'm quick and soaking, I reach under my bed, the floorboards darkening with a wet musty smell, and I grab my mosaic-work pliers. I pinch the metal fan switch right in the needle-nose and twist till the blades die out. I try to hold tightly to my picture of North's eyes, but we're laughing crazy, my hair as if cups and cups of water have been poured in a big cool bath. The rain still falls hard and we struggle with the old fan, get it to the floor and tug down the heavy windowpane.

Then we hear the shouts and running downstairs. There's an old fan like this in nearly every window. We run down the steps into people running left and right.

"This one! Get the kitchen! The equipment! Stop—Wait—Sorry!"

More rain and voices, nothing slacking off. Everything angry at first, but then melting. Sue in the spare room at the front of the house sounds out a yowl, like some cat, but it's laughter. We run to that room, and the knob on the fan has come off in her hand, too. Her peach housedress is drenched and her mousy hair pushed wet from her face to show her smooth marble forehead. We giggle, helplessly, and I do my needle-nose trick to shut down the whirls of rain. Sue slips into giggles too, arms hugging her chilled slick frame. We go back into the hall, Tracie and me—we feel like jumping in the puddles like children—there are *puddles* in the hallway!—but we try to help.

Tracie bumps into Jude whose glasses fly from his face.

"Oh no," he says, putting his hands right on her belly without thinking. "Have I hurt—" then turning beet red.

"She's fine," Tracie says and pats his shoulder.

He beams but squints without his glasses, which I get for him and then run for Wood's room where I know there's nothing but a candle and a blanketless bed to keep dry. I slam into a sopping-wet Carson in the doorway, my head beside hers so our arms go into an embrace from the force of our run. She is touching me—is she holding me? She is supple and bending, strands coming loose from her pinned-up hair, coils curly as mine and chaotic—her lace collar limp with rain.

Oh my.

"*Dammit!*" we hear from the Sanctuary. "*Dammit to hell!*" Carson's eyes go wide, and we all run in on the squishy paisley carpet, like bumper cars, sliding, a cluster of kids who should be shocked at Leonard's sudden foul mouth, but who cannot keep from cracking up at the sight of him with a handful of knobs from the three old fans sucking in torrents through each window, him going from one to another, doing twirls like he's dancing.

"The equipment!" he roars, and we get down to business, finding blankets for the taping machine and the speakers. And here's Omi Ruth to save the day with her pair of pliers. I twist and twist till the three fans putter to a stop, and Jude and Leonard get them down, shut the windows to the storm. We're a pack of drowned rats, softened—even Leonard, in his own way, swooping-back gray hair, still in surprise. For the rain was an utter surprise visit. Another rumble of thunder. The record heat relieved, our touching and bumping and clumsy dances all small embarrassments we don't seem sorry for. I hear us all panting in a funny restful rhythm. Do we go back to our own faraway corners now? No one is sure what to do.

And at the center of the room, the lamp has fallen.

Its stand, the skinny wooden box, has toppled to the floor, the lid popped off onto lake-wet paisleys.

Oh.

Old Loomis wanders into the Sanctuary from someplace—has she been napping? In her soggy nightgown, she goes right to the fallen box and sets it upright, as if trying to do her part to help. She looks down into the box and looks up at Leonard, then Jude, blinking like a baby who just woke up. "Why so empty?" she says.

My heart goes hollow.

Tracie looks for my eyes, but I turn fast and start to wipe Leonard's taping machine with a blanket edge. I think it's ruined.

"No, Sister Loomis," says Jude, still giddy. I look up to see his glasses on crooked. He walks over to peer into the Common Purse that I know to be emptied out. "Oh no," he mumbles. "Oh no."

"What is it?" Leonard's scowl is slinking back to his face; he wipes down his moustache.

Jude opens his mouth then shuts it. "It was all here. Sister Tracie's generous gift. After the bills were paid, I—" He swallows. "Has anyone taken from it? Sister Sue? Sister Carson?"

Shaking their heads. Then I'm not sure whether anyone looks at me because I'm back to studying the dial and switches and silver Sony letters on Leonard's equipment.

"How much was left?" Carson asks.

"Over two thousand, I think. Yes, over two thousand. Oh, Sister Tracie. Your gift—" I look, and Tracie has slipped out of the room. I'm stuck fast to the squishy floor till I hear Morse's truck chug into the alley. They're talking about calling a meeting, what to do, what to do about this. I tiptoe out, but I do see Jude's tear-filled eyes looking my way.

Up the stairs—what to do about this?—and into the closet-room, but she's not there. "Tracie? Tracie, are you here?" What will we do? My mind hums like an electric wire. They'll find out, and then what?

Out in the hallway, the chair sits in front of the bathroom door to say, "Leave me alone, I need privacy," but I don't think, I just barge in because what to do? What to say? Will they take the beautiful marker away from us? Through the door—

And it's her naked body.

Butterfly underwear, but all else naked. Her back to me. Her back. Her rain-wet leggings and sweater in a heap by the toilet. And her back that I have never seen before. She freezes. All her rainwater gone to solid pretty ice. In front of her, her hands have been wringing out her curls. Hair still pulled over her shoulder to show me all of her naked back.

Her back that has wings.

I cannot speak, she does not speak. I let the door slip and shut us in. Feathers on her shoulder blades, so tiny, outlined a dark blue. A million feathers. Along her spine, two small dark clouds where the wings join her tanned skin. Like where tree roots meet ground, then shoot up and out. Wings folded down, falling halfway down to her waist, feathers long as my fingers at the wingtips. Tracie Casteel? From Detroit? From darkness descending before the darkness? This strange day has somehow set us loose—we're floating.

And I am floating close, no gulf between us. I do not think, I just touch. She shivers once but not again as I trace the arc and leafy edges of the feathers. Dark blue shadows that cool underneath each one. Dark blue ink tattoo just like Odell's, his on the arm, a serpent and a busted heart.

She has hidden them inside sweaters all this time, but why? Why keep such pretty wings a secret? This feather and this feather and this? Like they're frail or something, or like they mean something she was not ready to explain, a woman with wings. Though I touch them, they fly her to the outer edge of my world, just beyond my reach, but this time I follow. This feather and this. So close that I wonder if the tattoo ink can rub off on my hand, so far that I cannot call her name. Just like Wood, grown up with happiness, right beside me but far far.

And it comes clear to me.

A case of my Clear Morning Mind here in the hot full bath in the late afternoon. I know the secret that flickers at the bottom of the well. I know it more surely than I know my own name.

"Things with wings," I whisper. Bats, planes, dragonflies— "Omi, I have something to tell you"—Golden eagles—A happiness like a grown man's—"Angels," I said to him and he heard. My whole hand now spreading over a wing to know its pattern.

"She's Wood's baby, isn't she?" I say. "You carry my brother's child."

Tracie turns and pulls the wings back into privacy. My hand still on her skin, on her chest bone now, her heart of thunder. She's puzzled how I know. I will tell her about the tractor, about our interrupted game, our near getaway in a plowed field.

"It's true?" I ask.

She nods, so lightly. "I'm sorry. I was gonna tell you, when I was ready."

I'm flooding inside like the rain is still blowing in. "An angel then?"

"No. Far from it. I got this trashy tattoo when Daddy left. I'll fly to him when Mama's mean, I thought." She looks down at her heap of clothes. "Wood liked it an awful lot. So I save it for just him to see. He did just like you, tracing the lines up and down. It tickles."

Her breasts are so large above her rounded belly, they touch me. The nipples dark dark eyes. I'm flooded with everything. It was her, up so early, slipping down to Wood's bed and lighting that candle. It was her and this baby that had grown his happiness, which I could not reach. It was her weeping when the baby chick drowned on the tape, her fingers on the chiseled wave of words on granite, *here he lies who wakes to sleep.* I have a million questions, but only one thing I need to know right now.

"Did he forget me? I mean, did he ever talk about me?"

"Oh, girl, every day. He loved you, natural as a fish loves water. Couldn't wait till I met you. He said we'd be good sisters."

Flood breaking loose into pure water and fish, color and light, my face on her bare chest like I'm a baby about to nurse, and she doesn't push me away.

We were a long time holding each other till Tracie twisted the rusty fixtures on the sink and we splashed our faces. I told her about the farm trip and the secret of her he meant to share, and she told me the story of a radio tryout in a Michigan town she couldn't remember the name of. It was a contest to be on the air—they needed singers for the jingle and a voice to announce the top hits. So there they were, she and Wood, strangers in the small crowd gathered outside the recording booth, making eyes and nervous as cats—things that I, Omi Ruth, surely didn't know, but it didn't make me sad to hear them, to let him be more than I could contain. She said he had a radio name he was proud of—Joe Woody Jax. I laughed and held the impossible name in my mouth, rolled it over and over, three smooth candies. Neither of them won a thing, she said, but they went out for root beers and he kissed her softer than anybody'd kissed her, there in the bus depot in some no-name Michigan town.

The bathroom is stifling and our rainwater has mixed with sweat. We pad over to our Big Top to change—me into cutoffs and a T-shirt, and Tracie into her sweater. "No," I say, "don't cover up again, I don't think he'll mind." I love her wings so much, I beg and beg till she puts her sweater aside. Out of her duffle she pulls tops I've not seen: tank tops, scoop-backs, spaghetti-straps—oh my, that bag is *bottomless*. "Yes, that one," I say to the light pink, gathered-to-a-rose pucker in front. Just strings for straps so the wings will flap free.

"They ain't gonna like it," she says, but she obliges. "'Specially Leonard."

"Shit," I say, then cover my mouth. Tracie raises her eyebrows. My fear ebbs back in with her mention of Leonard. "Oh, Tracie—the money. They'll take the pretty grave marker away."

"No, nobody's moving that headstone. Right? You hear me?"

Yes, nodding, I hear.

"They don't know who did it. There's lots of people could've stole that cash."

"Like who?"

"I'm working on it." She pulls her pink shirt on, flipping her yellow curls dry so the hoop earrings dangle. We're sisters, so close, like no two girls ever before. I'm so full of love, I have to work hard to stay worried. We sneak barefoot down the steps. The Sanctuary door is closed, but not latched, so we hang by the banister and listen.

"I warned you years ago, and it was God who warned me."
It's Morse Calhoun's thick voice.

"Brother Morse, it's not right." Jude sounds like a string
pulled taut.

"You didn't listen then," says Morse, "and look what happened. The city on a hill is surrounded by the wicked world.
If you don't lock it out, Jude, it creeps right in. *I* know. I work
with them, I hear their filthy talk."

"No one's stolen from us since the beginning," Sue says. We
can hardly hear her.

"There's a first for everything. And I hate to say it, Leonard,
but I'm the one working my tail off to put food on the table.
I deserve some respect. And what about Lucy?" Morse's voice
cuts. "You can't say we haven't sacrificed."

Chair feet rubbing the wet carpet. Leonard must be standing.

A hush, then Morse again: "I know you don't want to admit
it. But you think the same."

"What is it?" I whisper to Tracie. She shakes her head, shh,
rubs her belly.

"It's time we call the police," Leonard says. I picture him
stroking his neat moustache, feet planted. "I've seen the boy,
too, and he should be questioned."

"Fuck," Tracie lets out, a stab in my ear when she talks like
the Bueys.

"Who do they mean?" I ask her.

"He's fingering Reagan. Should've known it, that goddamn
Morse."

"So they don't think it was me?"

Other chair feet scooting. "It's not right, Brother Leonard,"
Jude says.

"Omi, we can't let them stick Reagan."

"How do you know they mean him?"

"Ain't too hard. We got to tell them."

"But they'll take the marker away. Tracie, you didn't see the little ugly one. You love Wood—you love him more than anything. And maybe that boy does steal. Maybe he does it other places and needs to get caught."

Her black pearls burn me. They hurt. I see Reagan's white shoes, hear his soft voice. I have said something very wrong. Reagan has sisters with hands in each other's hair.

"I'm sorry," I say. "Don't be mad. I'll tell them."

Her wings face away from me, they face up the stairs. I stand and head for the door.

"Wait," she says, her eyes still fire, but not burning at me now. "Let me do the talking."

"But I stole the money."

"Just let me do the talking."

We go in together. I picture the granite angel splitting away from the black heart with seventy-five letters carved, a little over seventy-five.

They're silent as we enter, all the men still standing and the three women folded into their chairs like soggy handkerchiefs. The awkward dancing we did here has all drained away with the rain, like it was years ago. The windows are still shut—even though the storm is over—and it's hot as a sealed tomb in here.

"Do you have something to say?" Leonard asks, filled to his brim with displeasure.

"I know you're gonna call the cops," says Tracie, "but no need." She pauses. I take her hand, ready for my punishment, but not ready to lose that grave marker. Jude's sadness shows as it runs down his cheeks. His eyes trail over Tracie even so; they drink in her skin that's newly bared. She puts the hand I don't hold on her hip. "It was me who took it."

A gasp from Carson, and I gawk at Tracie Casteel.

"Sister Tracie," Jude whimpers.

"Sister Tracie," I echo.

"Now, it ain't what you think. I had to steal it back, and let me say why. I made a phone call day after my check came. I felt real good dumping that cash in, you all's been like kin to me. I'm so thankful," hanging her head in a way I think is too dramatic. "But I made a call in to some family I still got up in Detroit. I know I didn't tell you about them, but I couldn't. They drink. Well, she drinks and he's in and out of jail. My aunt and uncle on my mama's side. I was calling just to check in, tell them I was good and cared for with a roof over my head, and she tells me she got medical bills climbing up the walls. I had no idea. It's cancer." She waits for that to take effect, wrings her hands together and *tsk-tsks*. "I had no idea, and my only family left." A real tear slips down her cheek. I can't believe it.

"Ah, now," Sue purrs. They're buying it. Morse sits down.

Tracie lets out a deep sigh and keeps going. "But they think they got it all, thank the good Lord. All them nasty tumors. She'll live, if only she can keep the bank from getting the house. She'd never burden me with that tale if she wasn't hurting, and, sure enough, I find out Uncle Pete's back in for six-to-eight, maybe more, so she ain't got nobody but me."

I remember that day I clutched dirty sheets to my chest, heading for the laundry, and this girl brought me the mail. Just like she'd brought mail to some lady in Detroit, spinning out a story to get herself some fried chicken. I mean, this Tracie Casteel can *lie*.

By the end of it, they're all sitting down. Jude's still weepy; Loomis wipes her eyes and struggles with a drip of snot.

"I'm so sorry I done this to you all. You been so good to me." Real tears again.

"Well. It's understandable," Leonard mutters. Leonard! I guess he'd look stingy if he didn't forgive her thieving. *My* thieving. "We'll have to discuss how to proceed then," he says.

"Oh yes, I know. I know," and Tracie pulls me by the hand back out the door. A little more sucking in of breath behind us: I know they see her tattooed wings. I grin wide.

We lie together on my tiny bed, squeeze in close and crack up.

"Did you see their faces?" I say. "And you were really crying!"

"I don't got an aunt living in Detroit. Hook, line, and sinker though." She gathers her curls up into a wild fountain on the pillow to give air to her neck.

"I guess I am a little nervous, Tracie. What do they have to discuss?"

"Who knows? Maybe how to send roses to my poor sick Aunt Mabel," giggling again.

"No, I mean it." I sit up. "They won't make you leave, will they? They can't."

She pulls me back down beside her and strokes my pestering rain-matted hair from my forehead. "No, I ain't leaving."

Of course. She'll stay by me.

We look up into our Big Top, and she says, "Besides. That Jude won't let me nowhere out of his sight."

"Jude? Why's that?" But I guess I already know.

"That man's in love with me. It's written all over his little-boy face."

Plain as day.

"They won't kick me out."

And she was right.

I'm at North's bed rail that night telling him the story. Whether Jude spoke up for Tracie or not, the C.P. decided to take no action. Morse would get his check at the end of the week, and we'd manage. Tracie vowed to offer up her next government wad and to call for a meeting before sending anymore aid to her aunt and uncle in Detroit, who would, of course, be mentioned in our next circle of prayer.

Just like that.

The angel hugging that dark elegant heart over Wood's grave and my own personal angel—I called her that though she denied it—beside me forever, her baby coming soon enough to join us. Baby Jax, we decided to call her, after Wood's radio name. Most everything's perfect.

Or almost perfect.

My North's eyes are closed again. I smooth his wild eyebrow, put the wet sponge gently to his lips. I think about his gray-green eyes, like stones that trap a bug inside—the amber I saw once with a mosquito locked in for millions of years, in *National Geographic*, but I don't remember where or why or how. Just the image of the stone-still wings.

I've taken to unbuttoning my cutoffs sometimes, when I'm here by him and I know no one in the house stirs, Jayne and Regina packed up for the night. Sometimes I slip my hand no farther than the waist of my underwear and slide my fingers back and forth. Sometimes I place his fingertip-eyes right on my tender chest, overtop my shirt, and move them slowly under my barely there breasts, in the place where, if my breasts were bigger and open to the sun like the divers', a shadow would smile its curve underneath. Sometimes I reach all the way down and feel for the vibration, in wet valleys like lips, growing soft hair around them. Just the *click whirr*, *hiss hmm* and my own soft *ahhh* when the full shudder, like a breaking bloom, comes.

But not tonight.

Tonight I just sit by him in my chair with my hands folded. I don't even feel the weak echo, the sweet tingle. I sense a small sorrow over my lack of feeling, and I stay by his side only because I feel that I should.

You need to let him go, said Regina to me. Two months now, and not much longer. I try to shake this pair of small sorrows by going to the closet to look for my sewing kit. And, yes, Jayne— or maybe even Regina—has folded all the dried-out fabric back into the cellophane. Tomorrow, I think, I'll cut the pieces and start sewing. I'll have to sew by hand, for Nancy took back her Singer machine.

The bedroom door opens behind me. I don't hear it, but a faint light spills in from the hallway, maybe from the bathroom.

"Sister Omi," softly, barely a whisper. Jude has come for me, but why?

I follow Jude down the stairs, my eyes on his shadowy shoes, into the empty kitchen. He pulls out a chair for me and switches on the little stove light so it's not too bright to shine under Loomis's door. Jude wears the work jeans and old shirt the rain soaked today. They wrinkle up in the light; I see how thin he is and how young; never before have I thought him so young. Just a boy now who thinks all the time on Tracie Casteel, like Wood had done. I start picturing Jude in his room at nights: he's on the bedside phone instead of reading his sacred, beautiful words; I hear him calling in on a request and dedication radio show, asking for a love song.

At the center of the table: the ceramic napkin holder in a chicken shape; the pair of salt and pepper shakers, each shaped like an egg; a few copies of *The Call*, the one on top with a close-up of cornstalks on the cover. The silk tassel makes me think of Tracie's mama's hair. Magazines clutter the house, now that I've quit cutting them up for collage. And next to the corn in tassel, two things not usually on the table. One looks like a photo album, but I've never seen it before. The other is a thick book with glittering gold letters that I *have* seen before: *A Memorial Collection of American Verse*. My heart that has been calm and plump and cool all evening heats up now and hollows out, like it did when I saw the skinny wooden box tipped over.

I listen hard for what love song he dedicates to her over the airwaves, but I can't hear it.

"Would you like some hot milk, Sister Omi?" He doesn't want to sit. It's still stifling in this house; thinking of hot milk makes my stomach churn.

"Maybe some ice cream," I say.

He shakes his head sadly. No, there's no ice cream, as if now we're on harder times than before. Our money is all gone, and also our little joys. Jude handles the photo album at its bent corners. I clasp my hands on the table and slip back into the curled cavern of my hermit-crab shell, looking everywhere but at that book of poems.

He sits down, diagonal from me, looking out the windows at his garden barrels in the darkness, but seeing only his reflection looking back. "The plants sure liked the rain today," he says and smiles secretly, for it was the rain that also bumped him into Tracie and placed his hand on her round belly without hesitation.

It occurs to me that Jude hasn't chosen to be a celibate man. It occurs to me to ask him about it, which flushes my cheeks. He rubs his neck and takes a deep breath.

"Sister Omi, I would like to share a few things with you. They're things you may not understand, but I think it's time you know them." Like he's reading my mind, like he's about to say, "No, I do not want to be a celibate man, I love Sister Tracie with all of my heart, and this song goes out to her." I lean closer to hear and push my hands farther toward the center of the table. I nudge the poetry book then pull back like it's a flame.

"I want to tell you about Brother Leonard and Sister Carson."

I'm surprised. What about Tracie?

"I know you're aware of the history of the Common Purse, that it was founded in 1965 with twenty-two families, led by the Wincotts, Cogdales, and Howards. That it filled Stephen House where the Bueys live now, and this Solomon's Porch and the Good Samaritan that's now an apartment building." He points as he says the house names like they're new to me. I start thinking he's the same as Leonard, giving a history of the C.P. for an interview but nobody's asking. "You know that we came here to live in harmony and simplicity, like the early disciples."

"I know. With all things in common, given out as each has need." And I don't feel guilt—haven't even once—only the flutter of fear that they'll swipe that grave marker.

"I know you've heard it before, Sister Omi, but maybe you can't imagine how wonderful it sounded to my broken heart when I was twenty years old. I came here in 1973."

"When I was born?"

"A little before then. I had a broken heart and a confused mind." His eyes are welling up.

"I thought you were always here, from the start."

"No, I came here because of Brother Leonard's kindness." Drying his eyes, and I lose some interest, hearing praise of my law-father. "He didn't always spend his time working on sermons for the Christian station. When the Common Purse began, more of the members had to work. Brother Morse was entry level at the plant and didn't earn what he does now. Brother Leonard's Mennonite foster family put him through seminary, so he got work as a chaplain at Hickory Hill. Do you know that place?"

What foster family? I shake my head no.

"Hickory Hill is a mental health clinic, and I was a patient there." He's looking at his hands, opening the photo album to the middle without paying attention. I'm not at an angle to see it. "I was obsessed with books as a young man, especially poems. So much so that I hid inside them. I loved the meter and rhyme and feeling, and I wanted to be a professor, but I hid from the real world. The world broke in, so to speak. I was at the university campus in South Bend and had a breakdown in here," tapping on his temple. He cries awhile. I'm used to waiting patiently for Jude's tears, but I'm eager now.

"Well, what happened?"

"Brother Leonard was the kindest soul I'd ever met. He prayed every day with me and told me about this fellowship where each person is equal and cared for and no one is alone."

I can hear Leonard's layer-cake voice, sweeter and sweeter on the outside but not so deeper down. Not so. "No one is alone," I say bitterly, like repeating some creed I'm forced to repeat. My tone hurts him.

"Things were—different—when I first came, that year you were born. It did feel like a family. Sister Loomis taught the homeschoolers with Sister Sue—there were eight children then and the houses felt so full of life. The boys ran from house to house throwing water balloons at everybody—Brother Wood-run too, even as shy as he was." Here I expect the tears to run, but no tears. He flips a page of the album, and in the light for a brief moment, I see a flash of a girl sitting on the ground, that's all. Breakdown, he said.

"What I mean, Sister Naomi, is that you should know *why* they started this place."

"I know why. God's orders." Then all I see is Wood with a squishy red balloon.

"No," he whispers. "Please come here." I scoot my chair next to his, and he's at the first page of the album, old brown photos like from a hundred years ago. "This is your father." He doesn't say law-father; he doesn't point to anyone I know. It's a young boy with sticking-up hair, cowlicks, in front of a dumpy house. He's dirty and far too skinny. I do recognize Leonard's planted tree-stump legs though, arms folded across his chest. "This was his younger sister, Elsie," pointing to the next photo.

I swallow hard.

The camera lens is tilted and up close to the girl Elsie, up in her face, like she holds the camera toward herself. She has swervy eyes, looking wild, ears not at the same height, like someone yanked one down too hard. Her mouth, just a few teeth—rotting or maybe it's the brown of the photograph—in a grin that scares me. I sit back in my chair.

He turns the page and it's the photo of Elsie sitting on the ground, the one I saw a flash of before. My, her legs are not right, the way they're bent. Another page and little-boy Leonard stands rolling a car tire, another and he and Elsie feed a deer. They play in a creek and her ruffled swimsuit's too small; I can tell it's secondhand like Lucy's clothes squeezing me. Elsie throws her head back—it could be a laugh, it could be a howl. My deep freezer opens and she steals inside.

"She was deformed from birth," says Jude to me, like he's talking about some other family than my own. "They lived in squalor—that was Brother Leonard's own word for it—outside of Indianapolis. He never knew his father, but his mother was violent. She couldn't handle Elsie's needs. When the girl died, the county came and took Brother Leonard away—he was eleven or twelve. They placed him with the Booth family, the parents of the farmer we visit in the spring, and they treated him like one of their own. In fact, they had quite a few foster kids, along with three natural kids, all treated equally. One of the natural kids was Sister Carson, his foster sister. They fell in love and decided to marry young, and after his seminary training, they outgrew the Mennonite farm—they had a vision for a city on a hill in the middle of town. The Booth family never had much money but what they had was shared, and they purchased the Stephen House and gave their blessing. After a few years, the fellowship needed more space, so the other two houses were bought." Jude keeps flipping pages. He's dry eyed but wistful.

I've quit looking at the photos. How strange I feel, like my feet and legs are in this kitchen but my head and arms are someplace else. Someplace where Elsie lived and died and where secrets keep coming out of the earth like steam from the *Geographics* geyser holes. Leonard's mama mean like Tracie's, Carson in love, Carson young? My head's so light, I don't feel it, but I guess I'm shaking it no because Jude stills me and says, "Yes. It's all true, Sister Naomi. And I don't need to tell you that things haven't gone well. It was hard to lose the houses, and so hard when Lucy was taken away and we were questioned by the child welfare office. People have moved out and died and have left us as a remnant. So many ghosts. And our fears have let poor judgment in." Is Jude talking to me or to somebody out in the garden where he stares? "And it has hurt Brother Leonard the most."

I see him in the creek with crippled Elsie, her swervy eyes, he held her hand. I see that. I squint to see it deep in my mind. Wood held my tiny hand on the banks of the Elkhart River. I wonder what headstone Leonard bought for her, if an angel watches over her, but he was a scruffy boy with no government check, so maybe he couldn't mark where she lay. I wonder, Is she buried way down in Indianapolis? Or someplace near Wood?

Jude reads my mind truly this time, still looking at the dark windows that only reflect back his ghostly young-man face in the stove light. "I wanted you to know the reason why Brother Leonard might keep things from you. And why he has turned hard." So quiet. It is difficult for Jude to say such a thing. "He misses his son so much. So much that maybe he wanted to get a nicer headstone than we could afford."

I look at Jude who looks at me squarely.

He knows.

He says, "We got an advertisement in the mail, from Meadow View Memorials, in your name, thanking you for your purchase."

Oh why hadn't Tracie taken in the mail each and every day?

"I overlooked it until the money came up missing."

"Please don't take it away," I whisper, holding tightly to my secret but Jude's prying my fingers away.

"I went to see it tonight," he says.

Dread inside, crippling me.

"It's very lovely." And he stands, folds up the old photo album in his arms. I understand his movement, that it maybe means the angel is safe in her place by the black heart. He backs away, turns off the little light over the stove and is about to disappear into his room where he may or may not call in a love song on the radio.

"Jude," I say, and he stops, his face in shadow. "I tore a poem from your book."

"I know," he says.

Maybe there is moonlight, or light from someplace hidden, but the gold lettering shines on the book's spine before me on the table.

I tiptoe upstairs into our room, suddenly so tired. Will I tell Tracie Casteel all of these millions of things that I now know after this strange day? All of this lifetime of knowing? But she is fast asleep, having left on the small lamp for me. She lies on her side, facing her green wall, in a silky nightgown that must have been way down at the bottom of her bottomless duffle bag. It's backless, showing most of her and letting the tattooed wings breathe. Beautiful, like maybe Wood saw her, in so soft a light as this. I ask her in my mind, Would you rather be beautiful or good? She'd answer, *Mmhmm?*, her noise that means, "You awake?" and "What's that again?" and "You remember?" and "Sure, sure, sure. Sure thing."

And I think maybe there's no difference between the two— being beautiful and being good. Or maybe you're one thing when you can't be the other. I slip out of my clothes and pull on my nightgown. I feel it touch every part of me. All of the things I know now have floated up to the surface of my skin. They are touchable and tender there, like my North's round, spreading bedsores. They hurt, but they can know the soothing salve, too.

OLD SOULS

I GET a cool cool morning on October 1, a gift for my birthday. Today I'm thirteen, and Tracie has done up my hair with the slick pomade I love, even though it's given me pimples on my forehead. She's seven months now, too big to get comfortable on the front stoop, so she sits on my bed, with me on the floor, and pieces out each strand and hums to the radio. I don't know how or when, but she bought me a box of barrettes for my birthday, with silver sunflowers on the tips; she's clipped them in a curve over my head, like a tiara, she said.

These days, Tracie and me, we're inseparable. We thought about telling Carson and Leonard whose baby Tracie's carrying, but she said, "Only one shock at a time." And it's true they don't care for her tattooed back. Maybe they'll get used to it. I think Sue even likes it; she's never had ideas for art projects, but she does love beautiful things. She loves to look at old paintings, like the ones in the book of postcards that Lucy got her once at the museum in Indianapolis. I watch Sue watch the intricate details of Tracie's blue-ink feathers when she moves. And of course Jude loves them, but Morse doesn't like them at all; his face goes dark when she's in the room, but he may just be returning the dark arrows she shoots at him.

Tracie's too big to wear her skimpy spaghetti-strap shirts—they slide up to show her belly—but I made a fuss to see her wings, so she finally asked Nancy Calhoun for that sack of sundresses. Now Tracie flows through the house like water and wind. I watch her flow down the stairs, holding the banister; the longer dresses trail behind like a queen's train, a queen who wears sure black boots and silver hoops. She has somehow spread her wings over me, and I feel, at times, invincible.

But I still don't leave the house to walk the streets of Dunlap.

It's difficult to explain why. It's not fear—for didn't I go clear to the cemetery for our private funeral? And it's not my hermit-crab shell. It's more about responsibility. It's age and busyness. Carson will ask me to go to the post office with her, to mail in her correspondence work, or Sue will want me along to get school supplies. But I say, "No, I'm too busy."

I wasn't sure for a while whether Wood's soul was still in me or not—no flutter, so I thought maybe he's finally resting with his granite angel. But now I think his soul's just growing old with mine, mine and North's. Tracie's soul seems to get younger, for she carries two, one belonging to Baby Jax. Nancy says it's good for Tracie to walk, so she'll do three times around the block and ask me to come. "No," I say, "you go on, I have something," and that's when I work on her baby blanket. Then Jude offers to walk with her, and sometimes she'll take his arm—I see that from the window. I watch her wings and his narrow shoulders till they make the corner, and I wonder if I've skipped all the in-betweens in life and, if so, will I regret it when I'm lying there like North—with a million years shining up through my paper skin—and no longer thirteen? Will my years even shine through if I spend them all haunting the stairs and hallways of Solomon's Porch? I go to North's bed rail, with my needle and thread; I smooth his eyebrow and hear his clock ticking, like Regina says it's ticking—he's going on four months now—and I watch his inner years, trusting them. Some of them wild, some horribly sweet, all of them a mystery—and my own?

But with my grown-woman responsibilities, I don't have time to ponder long because I'm apprentice midwife, I'm nurse to a man between living and dying, and I'm as much a hotel keep as Jude. For I'm full of the lives of this house—and of the other two houses, too—full of the twenty-two families who joined the fellowship then turned to ghosts, full of Leonard's photo album of hurts, of Reagan's sisters, of Chastity's chain-smoking, of Odell's ugly snake tattoo with fangs eating up his forearm. Of even the hotel guests that linger from long ago, each one clasping a skeleton key from a time when every door had a keyhole. The Common Purse is not only the remnant Jude said it was; it's a fellowship in full operation—it's just operating inside of me now. It's a lot of work to keep it up, so what time do I have to go out to the grocery or post office or hardware, or to Cindy Lane's for a Coke?

I'm making good progress on my blanket. Only a few more rows left. And since I sew beside North, I often say, "You go on, Jayne, and do your errands, I'll watch," so now I'm more hours with him. I hardly use the pillow-slip pattern anymore; I've made it my own: four big blocks in each row, all different widths but the same height. I make the red block last in one row, then third in the next, then second, then first, then last again, so it's a streaking diagonal of red doing a zigzag. It felt funny, cutting up Wood's shorts—I left both back pockets on, where he would have carried his radio, so that, if she likes, Baby Jax can slip something in when she's swaddled up. Out of the blue, Carson brought me a yellow scrap for my blanket, from an old pretty tablecloth. I don't know how she knew I was sewing; she folded it into my hand at evening prayer circle, which is another thing I've grown less childish about. I've quit the game with the shoes and I try to pray along with Leonard—partly because when he prays I can glimpse the skinny boy with cowlicks now and then, rolling a tire, but mostly because of how I've grown older. I'm formal and sad and faithful, and I think: my North is the Man I Love who used to walk the world like I did, but no longer. I find comfort in him, comfort but no more shudder, no pleasing tingle. No fire.

Only sometimes, as I salve North's sores, do I stop to look over at Vaughn's black shade to see it raised up. And I wonder, does he know I'm thirteen today? One night, as I waited on the back steps for Tracie and Jude to get back from a stroll, I sat in shadow and here came Vaughn's car just missing me with its headlights. He must have had a day off since he'd usually be on shift at that time. The passenger door opened, the dome light came on, and I saw a girl's head beside his, leaning one way then the other, and his following hers like they were tied together with string, her straight straight hair in a wagging ponytail. I heard her giggle, and the door shut some but not all the way. Then they were no longer upright, they'd ducked down. I knew they were doing more than touching each other's legs.

Earlier that day I'd gotten a little blood on my cutoffs when I'd left my Always pad on too long, so Tracie had lent me the sheer green sundress from Nancy's collection, the one with a scooped back, and I'd shaved my legs again because blacker hairs had grown prickly all over and it had burned like fire just as badly as before, and the pimples had started on my forehead. So I didn't wait around to watch Vaughn's car rocking. I went over to my mosaic wall, in the green dress that was too long, and I touched one jagged piece then another—I knew it pearly blue, I knew it brown, I knew it gold flecked—seeing only in the way North sees, by fingertip, for it was dark and I was trying to find the young Naomi Ruth Wincott who had stood there dreaming up a curve of wing before she'd grown old and old with the Time of Loss. A part of me knew I was being dramatic, like I was playing a part, but I stayed solemn. Maybe I'm waiting to see what will happen to my life.

And what of Spencer Frye, I think sometimes. I wonder, did I scare him off, hitching that ride with Tracie in his buggy, because he has not been back with another sack of radishes. I asked Chastity one day in the backyard, "Is he still bussing at the diner?" And she said, "Yes, do you want me to tell him hi for you?" "No," I said, "that's okay." But maybe she did it anyway because, twice after that day, I found a bundle of black-eyed Susans on the back steps, tied with yarn. Roots balled up into wet paper towels with care.

Besides all my responsibilities, the home school has started up again, on *top* of the twice-a-week Lamaze training Nancy gives us. It was my idea to get Jude to teach us literature, and he agreed in a flash. To teach Sue, too, because all she really knows naturally is mathematics—that, and she's really good at memorizing and saying back all the information on the back of her art postcards while she holds them up for us to see.

One morning Nancy was going over how to not hyperventilate when in labor. We had read that chapter already, and Tracie beat her to it. "Put a paper bag over your mouth," she said. "Mama did that often enough."

"Good, good," Nancy said, clucking like a hen and going right into the next step, how to do the light massage of the belly. "Just gentle *effleurage*," she said, demonstrating on Tracie, "a pleasing distraction for the laboring woman, according Dr. Fernand Lamaze."

I noticed Jude watching the gentle *effleurage* in the doorway of the Sanctuary, and I smiled. Nancy saw him and got huffy— "It's a private session," she said. He muttered something about being early for the poetry lesson and then hurried off.

"So he's giving lessons, is he?" *Cluck, cluck.* Wearing her tragic face. "Don't you know, girls, that man was going to be a professor? He was on track, a real scholar, and the fool threw it all away to join a half-wit commune. You girls have got to shoot for something bigger."

I thought Tracie would get mad at that, but she was too tired, so I said, "Oh, don't you know, Miss Nancy? He didn't throw it all away. He had a breakdown," tapping my temple, "in here." She huffed at me.

My favorite art postcard of Sue's was by Edgar Degas, spelled with an *s* but said without it. He's known for his ballet dancers, Sue said, and she had some of his girls in pink tutus, but my favorite was the laundresses. Two red-haired women working hard, like me when I wash and fold North's sheets and towels and nightshirts. One's bending down pressing a sheet; the other's rising up for a stretch and a yawn, wearing a pretty yellow scarf, arms thick. When Jude saw that I liked it so much, he showed me a poem in a new book he'd mail-ordered at the bookshop in South Bend—Boland, an Irish woman poet, with a poem called "Degas's Laundresses" that Jude said was about that very painting. He let me borrow the book—as if he'd forgotten I'd torn a page from his *Memorial Collection*—and I copied out by hand the beginning and end, for I don't care much for the middle of poems. I just love the way they start, like they're getting the attention of your soul, and the way they end in a whisper, saying a secret. It said: "You rise, you dawn roll-sleeved Aphrodites," and I felt the two of them rise and yawn, though I didn't recognize the *a* word. And at the end, the last line: "It's your winding sheet." I did go to the middle to find out what *it* was and *it* was *his mind*. Whose mind? I looked farther up and *his mind* was the painter Degas's mind. The painter whose laundresses these were, but he did not own them, I didn't think. Not their coiled-up red hair, not their strong arms. How could he? I looked on Jude's Bible commentary shelf till I found a Webster's and I looked up *winding sheet*. A shroud, it said. A sheet for wrapping a corpse. "Oh," I said out loud; the poem was changed for me, it went darker, and I breathed fast for some reason, thinking maybe I'd need a paper bag to calm down, but I didn't. I rose to stretch and yawn; I listened to the whisper telling its dark secret to me.

One more responsibility fell to me: to get some order in the magazines that littered the house. When Jude canned his jam and beans and tomato sauce, he asked, could he use pages from *The Macedonian Call* to cushion the jars in the storage crates? "Yes," I said—like I was boss—but not the *National Geographics*, for they show all the earth and not only the places the missionaries have designs for. So Jude said we should put the *Geographics* in chronological order and on display for the home school, and, with clearness of mind, I knew right where to put them: on top of the soaked taping equipment that Leonard had tried to fix but was shot. It had no use beyond a sturdy surface. Jude gave me two metal bookends from his shelves, each in the shape of a horse's head. I even brought down my favorite magazines from under my bed, like the India feature, though it had holes where saris had once been. But not the ama divers; that one I kept stashed with my folded picture of beautiful Asma, my postcard from Coal Lick, my save-the-day mosaic pliers. I displayed 1979 up till now, all standing straight between the metal horse-head weights, a neat row of yellow spines. Then Jude said he had ones from the earlier seventies in his room, and could I bring them out?

I found the stack on his nightstand under the phone. I hefted them and of course got curious, spilled them onto his bed and started looking for the one on the endangered baby seals I once saw so I could show Tracie how pretty and near lost they were. But my collage-making hands took over and plucked up an issue from 1970 with "Retrospective" in big white lettering and, underneath that, "World Press Photos of the 1960s." Several mini pictures made up their own neat collage along the border of the cover. I cleared away the other *Geographics* and sat myself on Jude's bed and opened to the middle.

Right away I wished I hadn't.

A man on fire, sitting still as a stone. A wild movement of black and white flames. Movement of other men in robes walking to the edge of the picture, leaving him. I could not close it, my deep-freezer lid stuck open wide. An old-time car behind him with its hood up like its engine had blown, a million people watching. Robes and robes. If I couldn't shut it, I'd look hungrily for words surrounding it. "By Malcolm Browne," it said in slanted print under the photo. "1963. Saigon"—a city I did not know—words on the opposite page. A Buddhist monk—Buddhist, I thought, didn't Buddhist mean not calling on God?—fellow monks poured gasoline on him and he set himself ablaze. Silent protest. Never moved a muscle. Four rolls of film. Then I was rubbing up and down my legs, feeling my skin on fire under Gillette shaving cream, the closest thing I could imagine.

I heard a throat trying to clear.

It was Old Loomis in the room with me, coming out of nowhere in her flannel nightgown that looked like their robes. Clearing her throat again, she sat by me on the bed, right on top of a magazine cover of red desert dunes, and she looked where I was looking. Just me and her. She spooned up some jam from one of Jude's jars that she held; she nibbled and slurped and cleared her throat, all her secrets gummed up in the food she couldn't quite digest. I knew Leonard's secrets now, Carson's, poor Elsie's, and I somehow knew hers too. Her hair needed washing. She dropped the spoon on the floor and took my hand, me the grown woman and her the child, and we held hands looking at this man burning himself alive on the streets of Saigon.

Only two issues are missing in the thick row of magazines that line the top of the busted recording machine and speakers. The divers and the retrospective. Nobody has noticed they're missing but me.

These silver sunflower barrettes might be my only birthday gift, but I won't know till lunchtime when Jude brings out the cake. It's a painful wait till then, for it's Hospitality Sunday when we have a guest preacher and open the doors to all of Dunlap. Leonard invites a speaker once or twice a year; he chooses one from the county directory of preachers and sends a formal letter. He's still giving his sermons all the other Sundays, but since the recording equipment is beyond repair, Leonard sometimes repeats sermons now, instead of writing new ones—I recognize the endings, when he spins a little hit-home story that's meant to make you feel bad enough to repent and vow to do better.

Leonard's got a stack of fliers: "Hospitality Sunday" in an arc of blocky letters, information listed below like a party invitation with "Who," "What," "When," "Where," and then blanks that he fills in. It's a Xerox of the same one every time, so the blocky letters are getting faint and hard to read. He puts fliers in mailboxes, or hands them out on the corner of Tyrone and Jackson, sometimes farther out; he puts a stack on the stoop of the apartments next door. Today's "Who" says that "Pastor of Shalom" is coming to preach, and we've never had him before. The preachers always come from the Mennonite churches, white-haired men who all sound the same: "Good morning," they say, hand in a cup by their ear, "I said Good *morning*!" and we say "Good morning!" as loud as our remnant can because it's never anybody but us, the C.P. people. Never a big crowd of strangers, or even a handful. I hope Pastor of Shalom talks fast and is hungry for dinner; they always stay for Jude's meal and take two helpings of everything. Leonard scowls at that, even on Hospitality Sunday.

I'm the first one in the cool Sanctuary. Despite the October chill, I've worn the green sundress again, and since I'm Miss Omi Seamstress these days, making my secret blanket, I've hemmed the skirt. A little crooked, but not bad. My legs are shaved birthday smooth. Tracie comes in to sit by me, wearing an orange dress I love, with tiny seahorses on it; the seahorses stretch taller over her big belly. One of my silver sunflower barrettes has come loose, so I'm fixing it when I see a lovely purple hat come through the doorway.

My.

An old dark dark-skinned woman with bright white gloves, a lavender skirt and top, and that *hat.* Do I recognize her? Yes, from the apartments, because I've seen the woman behind her, a tall beautiful black woman in a smart pantsuit with her arms out ready to catch the older lady if she topples, which she looks like she may do. Then I can't believe it: it's two twin girls in lime-green taffeta dresses with their hair up in a spray of tiny black braids, lime clips at the tips. They have Reagan's oval face, and, yes, there he is, in his slow-dip walk—in a suit and tie! And those same Nike sneakers. They're the first guests we've ever had for Hospitality Sunday. I look around for Morse, nervous since he's not kind to Reagan, but he follows Sue in, calm as can be and looking straight ahead, like it's all business as usual at the C.P., like there are no strangers at all gathered in our half circle of chairs and dressed for some magnificent event. Jude—I notice him back in the home-school corner—dabs a cloth to his eyes.

A short black woman walks in, or more like limps with one foot not turned exactly straight ahead, as if it's trying to get away from her. Wearing a sky-blue dress that makes her look young, but she's not. There's a podium that Leonard brings out for visiting preachers and she walks right up to it, barely tall enough to lean her elbows on its wide wooden surface, and flashes a huge smile that spreads her lipstick-lips wide.

In come Carson and Leonard, and his brow scrunches. Feet planted sure as cement. "Pastor of Shalom?" says Leonard in his layer-cake voice.

The short woman clasps her hands on the podium. "You must be Brother Wincott," she says." "Pastor Shalom Mavis McDonald." She unclasps and limps over, goes in for a handshake. "They don't print me quite right in the county directory. Pleased to be here with you folks."

Leonard shakes her hand somehow like a teen boy.

"Glad the Lord woke us up to be here this morning," like her voice is on megaphone.

He nods and sits between Carson and Loomis, checking to see whether his gray moustache is still there.

The little sisters in taffeta have sat beside Tracie. One of the girls is up on the chair with her white shiny shoes and lacy socks, standing and bending to touch Tracie's feathers without asking. Tracie closes her eyes, I know she loves it. Reagan picks the girl up gently, his hands in her armpits, and sits her on the seat with a "behave now," soft, and an apology to Tracie, even softer. I think I see him look at Morse who does not look back.

"Come here, little lambs," says Pastor Shalom Mavis McDonald to the twins. Her black skin glows; she wears starry earrings I like. "Jesus's little lambs," and they shyly go up, hiding behind each other. She bends down and gathers them, lime in sky blue, into her chest, big and pillowy as Jayne's. I want to be little, I want to be tiny and held. "*A-ay-men*," Pastor sings, "*a-ay-men*." The girls slip back to their chairs. White-lace ankles dangle above the paisleys. "Come on—*a-ay-men*." No fake "Good morning," hand cupping the ear, "I can't hear you"— just straight song, as if we do this all the time.

But not one of us can sing, I think to her.

"*Amen, O Lordy! Amen, have mercy.*" Pastor Shalom raises her broad arms in a stretch and yawn, except her yawn bowls out song. "*Amen, amen, a-ay-men. Sing it over now.*" Parts of the half circle sway, just a bit, and Reagan joins her first.

Amen, O Lordy!

Amen, have mercy.

Amen, amen, a-ay-men.

Then again, in unison like a choir, all the strangers sing it loud. Then again, each time sounding new—how many ways you can sing it? Then again, and I see Carson's lips moving, Sue's. Swaying like reeds by water with two stiff stumps in their midst: Morse and Leonard. Okay, but not me, I sway. Tracie's voice hurries to catch up with theirs, and mine's trailing after, off-key. Then it's Pastor Shalom on her own, but lifted by a bed of *hum* in the room:

See Him in a temple

talking to the elders.

How are they marveled.

Amen, amen, a-ay-men.

Almost everybody coming back in on that last part together. It's the first time I wish Leonard's taping equipment weren't ruined. Again we sing it, a million times again, each time sounding like a surprise, but always with a little sandpaper, rubbing up against Tracie's gospel voice, like she's been waiting for them. And everyone seems to know when it's over; even the hum-bedding thins out, then disappears, allowing Pastor Shalom's strong preaching voice to make its way alone.

"That's right," she says. "We can praise him anytime, anyplace. My grandson runs fullback for the high-school team in Gary. I was at the game Friday night and they were losing bad, but you know that sun started to set, and I don't know how the sun was setting that night in Dunlap, but oh over that football field it was a riot of color like I've never seen. Blues, pinks, indigo, gold. I stood up in the stands—I couldn't help myself—and said 'Praise *God*!'"—

Her arms stretching wide again, and she chuckles.

"My daughter yanked on my sleeve, saying, 'Sit down, Mama,' she was so embarrassed. The cheerleaders all looked up at me like I was a loony, and I said it again, 'Praise God and just you *look* at that sky!' and my other grandson who's too smart for his own good, he started grumbling. 'It's just pollution that makes it look that way, Gram, chemical reactions.' 'Well, so what,' I said to him. 'God can work with that, God can make something out of nothing, amen?'"

Amens coming through on the tin can, loud and clear.

"Yes, they marveled. How they marveled. Indeed. The elders who thought they knew it all—everything a closed book. Old man Nicodemus came to Lord Jesus at night—you know the story—he came sniffing around for some truth. Lord Jesus says to him, 'You must be born again to see the kingdom of God,' and Nicodemus, he gets confused. 'How can an old man be born again,' he asks—'how can he climb back up into his mama's womb?'"

Making her arms like they're climbing a ladder. The twins giggle and squirm.

"'Marvel not,' says Lord Jesus, 'marvel *not* that I say you must be born again.' Well, Nicodemus, he's scratching his head, like a little boy doing math that's hurting his brain—how can it be? Sweet Jesus pities the old man—he's a man who's done everything right, followed all the rules and not one misstep, dotted all the *i*'s and crossed all the *t*'s, but born again? How can it be? 'Born of the Spirit,' says Lord Jesus, 'for you will be like the wind, blowing wherever it wishes to blow. They'll hear you blow by, but they won't know where you come from or where you're going when you're born of the Spirit.'"

She's swaying like that wind. "We're getting closer, mmhmm?"—sounding just like Tracie does—"we're getting closer to being born."

Amens softer, unasked for, in the tin can, and I shiver.

"I had a real good birth," says Pastor Shalom, "into the thick arms of my mama's love. I had a good birth and I'm planning a good death, too. Just making my way back, with my tired soul. That's all living is. Nothing to fear, is there? Not a thing. Lord Jesus says, 'You've been working so hard, Nicodemus, like you're working for a wage—you can't earn my love, son. You can't earn what I give out for free.' That's why we're here today, is it not?"

She's leaning over the podium looking deep into our eyes, all of our eyes at once. Her eyes pierce; her short curls coil more tightly to her head; golden-star earrings wink in the light. I don't know about Jesus, but I think this woman loves me, just like that. So easy.

"We've come out for the milk and honey that flows free. We give no tight-lipped refusal! We lay down our hammer, our nails—we give up the six days of labor and sweat and climbing that steep hill, because we don't have to work hard for that love, no. Born of the Spirit, free as wind. I know it's been rough, I know. Lord Jesus knows." Then she's humming another song, so calm, and limping a step side to side, like she really does know. She knows I'm thirteen today. She knows I'm already a million years old. She knows everything here: what Tracie calls Morse, what happened long ago deep inside of Lucy Calhoun; she knows Jude is in love and she knows what the long white gloves on the old woman's hands have held tightly; she knows there were radio shows and, before that, hotel guests looking up from the TV, out the window, watching the world pass by on Tyrone Road. How does she know?

I can't explain my face wet with tears. I wipe my nose then wipe my hand on my green dress. I grow lost in the sound of her humming voice, and in the words she has preached out like a fountain. I'm inside her sound like I was inside Leonard's the day he preached Wood's burial and I dug hard, with a pickax through rock, to reach the deepest layers of his sedimentary stone. But I don't dig hard now, her sound just sweeps me away. Her sound is layered, too, but not in a cake or in pressed rocks, but in a picture I can't form for sure—it's like clouds, so many colors that mix with the smokestacks of Gary, Indiana; it's wind, rain, color, but grittier, so hail, too— or dust storm? No, sandpaper like Tracie Casteel's, doing what sandpaper does: smoothing, but with almost no effort. I look over at Leonard and his stiff-stump self, thinking that's not how he loves me; he loves me like it's a chore. Not easily, not the way he held Elsie's hand at the creek. And how do I love him? How easy it would be for him to take my hand, or for me to take his. More layers to her sound as her humming grows into words.

"*Wade in the water, wade in the water, children, wade in the water.*" There is Moses and the Holy Ghost and Jordan's stream, and I hear but I don't hear, my green dress wet and dark down the side where I wipe my hands that wipe my face. The song goes and goes. We wade and God troubles the water. So old, we're nearly born, as if that is the simplest, truest, most high-up thought in all the world.

Then everyone is up shaking Pastor Shalom's hand, then each other's hands. Reagan shakes Morse's hand like soft leaves shaking petrified wood. I hear Jude ask everybody to stay for the hospitality dinner, there's plenty, but no, they say. Pastor Shalom has an engagement at another church, and the family nods a thanks and slips out, heading back across the alley, though I hear the twin girls say, "Can we, Mom?" maybe because they smell the birthday cake Jude has baked. My tears have stopped. I touch my silver sunflowers.

It's only me and Tracie left in here. I look at her and, for the first time in a long time, her sadness curves her back, so severely it looks like she's fallen asleep over her seven-months-along belly. But I know she's awake. I want to ask what's wrong. Before I can, Tracie says, "I knew a pastor like her in Detroit. A woman who sang and said things just that sweet even though she'd lost everything."

"What did she lose?" I ask.

"Everything." Tracie sounds like I'm bugging her by sitting here, which stings me a little. I thought she'd put her arm around me when I was crying before. She says, "My daddy lost everything, too, that's why he was a big ball of hurt. The only black man in Coal Lick."

"Your daddy was a black man?"

"Something wrong with that?" She's clouding over me, about to storm—why? I suddenly worry that Baby Jax will look black and not like Wood, not with Wood's eyes and mine, and I'm mad that she's never told me.

"Of course not," I say, but she's not listening. I'm ashamed of my thought.

"Press Casteel. He sang these songs, too, before his lungs started filling. You know why I get such a big government check?"

I shake my head no, but she's not looking.

"Because Mama fought the government long and hard for black-lung benefits. She got me the years of back pay before she died. A dime for every breath they stole. These aren't songs for people like Morse Calhoun. People like him would've took a swing at my daddy in the tunnels and spit in his lunch pail."

I see it in her now, her tanned skin and kinky curls with dark dark roots. Strange and beautiful in a way I'm not. I think she'd rather go home with Reagan and his sisters and switch houses. I worry she's going to leave me.

"Come on," I say. "Let's go see my birthday cake."

Her look breaks me in pieces. I've said something wrong. I've lost her.

"You don't know nothing about the world, Omi. You're just a sheltered little girl."

"I am not. I know all about the world."

"What do you know about it?"

It's her sadness talking, I tell myself, and not meanness, but I'm getting hot.

"Lots of things," I say.

"Like what? Things in them magazines? You ain't ever set foot out of Dunlap. You don't hardly leave this house!" She stands and grips the tall seahorses at her middle, like she's in pain.

I stand, too, but I can't speak. Heat from my legs up to my eyes. No tears. Where is my sister?

"Do you know what it's like to have a mama and daddy die and leave you on the street? Then lose the father of your child?"

"He was my brother!" I shout.

"He couldn't wait to get out of this damn place. It's full up with spite!"

"No wonder your daddy left you." It's out before I can stop it. No, no, no. I've cut her.

"At least my daddy took me up in his arms—I'd rather he leave me than treat me like something that don't feel!"

"You're a liar—you lie about everything!" Am I shouting or whispering? Am I spinning?

"I'll say one thing for sure—you stink like that dying man! Like cow-udder cream and like the dead. He's already dead."

Heat rains from me, my eyes, my underarms, the bottom of my feet. My bones burn. "Your baby's going to have swervy eyes!" I scream. "And a crooked face and twisted legs!"

Then I know I spin. For she has slapped my face.

I am a green scoop-back dress flying up the stairs, flying to the Big Top that is no more a Big Top, just an ugly closet-room. I fly back and forth like the trapeze girl in silver and feather, except that I fall, right to the hard floor, and I grope around under the bed until I find it. I tear the soft postcard into tiny pieces. I am so lost, alone now because she will leave me. Everything slipping away. I want to talk to the angel holding the black granite heart, but I have no way to get there, I am trapped in this house. Then I stand and sober up. I will not cry. I am not crying. I am a grown woman and I don't need her. If she's leaving, then I'll leave first.

I will show Tracie Casteel what I know about the world.

DARK BEFORE IT'S DARK

I go for the blue and white polka-dotted party dress. I've hung it on a nail and not worn it since our grave visit. The picture of us holding each other in the morning dew shoves into my head, but I shove it back out. I shed one dress and slip into the other, buckling the thin white belt and pulling on the red shoes. I want red, I see red. There in the front pocket of the duffle, in the plastic pouch, I steal the lipstick tube. I've learned it's so easy to steal. I clasp it, then open my window to the cool October air, take out the screen as if I've done it a million times before though I haven't. But I've seen Jayne do it in North's room. I think then: I should tell him good-bye. I feel a flash of fear. No. No need to say good-bye, I comfort myself, I'll see him before dark.

"I'll see you," I say to the window screen that I leave on my bed. There is the busted air conditioner in the apartments across the alley—do the lime-dress twins live in that room? I wish the window were empty and clear. I wish they could see me now. And there is Morse's truck right under me. A wide cement ledge goes all around Solomon's Porch, and I can reach it with my red shoe soles just barely, hanging onto the windowsill. I feel the ledge, I scuff, then I feel it for sure. I'm on it, squatting, and I dangle my legs till I feel the top of his truck cab. I'm close to the kitchen windows, but I duck and nobody sees Omi Ruth run like lightning through the stacked, empty garden barrels, up the Bueys' back steps and through their screen door torn full of holes.

I'm inside hearing my breath and nothing else till I walk—light *click* of my shoes. I go through the hours in my mind: Odell's motorcycle not back till two, Chastity not back till four, it must be late morning still. Vaughn still in bed with the black shade down. I smell cigarettes and hotdogs. Dishes heap over in the sink; a pretty rag rug is crumpled; there's the scar in the linoleum the rug used to cover. I've been in here before, getting a Popsicle from Chastity, but I go to the stairs that I've not once climbed. I don't switch on the light, but I can see chips of white plaster on one step, two, six steps.

Do I knock? I breathe three times, and, no, I put my hand on the knob. My, it's the same fine old crystal. Stephen House this was, where a young Carson and Leonard first made their city on the hill. I open the door.

Vaughn's foot sticks out from under the blanket. The room is mostly black, just shapes of things till I get used to the dark: a lamp, a race-car poster, closet door open to a black hole. He sleeps like the dead.

"Vaughn," I whisper.

Nothing.

"Vaughn," louder, "it's me."

His bare foot steals back under the blanket, and I move in closer.

"Vaughn!" and he bolts upright, swinging his arm to punch something. "Vaughn, it's me."

"Holy shit—Omi? What the hell?" He scratches his hair. His whole chest and arms seem to pulse, seem frail.

"Vaughn," I say. "Take me out on the town." Not so dark now. The inside of the black window shade has an eagle on it.

"Do what? I just got to bed."

"Take me out on the town like you said."

Rubbing his eyes, looking at me now. A slow dangerous smile on his lips and he shakes his head. "Oh me, oh my. You're dressed to kill," says Vaughn to me. "Do I know you?"

"Come on, Vaughn. Don't tease. You know me."

"Come here. A man needs his rest—come barging into my room like some goddamn ghost. Omi Wincott here by my bed," shaking his head again. He's sleek, he's got designs, he's a hoodlum but he did like I asked with that gravestone, so maybe he's still as gentle as that boy who watched the hickory get cut and didn't know how to grieve over it. "Let me look at you." He holds out his hand.

I still clasp the lipstick tube. I'm dressed to kill, so I slip the cap off, make a skinny *O* and spread it thick. Then I walk closer to him, my red shoes making the light *click* that I like. I smell his smoke and the RV plant smell, motor oil and steel. He takes my wrist and pulls and I spin a little.

"Just look at you," he says, my back to him so I see his dark closet is full of work shirts. I feel his finger trace the back of the dress along my skin, then his whole hand on my low bare back—where Spencer touched, briefly, that time he claimed he'd taken me to church, me and Tracie who has slapped me and who's long gone now.

"We could just stay here," Vaughn's saying, his fingers slipping just inside the dress. Vibration and heat. I back up toward him, sudden but slow, eyes on the name patches I can

just barely make out on the shirts in the closet, and my movement moves his hand farther inside my polka-dotted dress, his
curving hand on the skin over my ribs. I think he trembles,
I'm amazed that I don't. "Hey there," he says, pulling me just
a little closer, a single *click* of my shoe, and if there was sun, if
there was a shore by the sea in this room, the shadow would
smile there, under my small breasts where North has seen with
his fingertips, where Vaughn touches and I feel a callus on his
hand. Other hand on my pleated dress skirt, down and down
to the hem, to my bare leg, then upward, past my knee—so
smooth this time, not little-girl legs, smoother than silk—on
the inside of my thigh and so close to the valleys I know are
wet like dew. I close my eyes.

Then, "Hey," he says when I float away slowly toward the
closet shirts, my whole self boiled up to my very skin that feels
every inch of my party dress. I throb.

"Not till you take me out on the town," I say, still facing his
closet, still feeling, with my eyes shut, what low moan might
come out from its hiding place inside my throat.

"Cruel, girl," he says. "You are cruel and you are strange." I
hear him flop back on his bed, the springs creaking. He laughs
but I still feel his trembling. Today I am cruel. He's right. Tracie is walking away and all I see is wings, I see them till they're
too small to see. Where will she walk to—Detroit?

"I'm thirteen now," I say.

"I know. Happy birthday." I hear him get out of bed. I sense
his near nakedness till he pulls on his cloth work pants. I turn
around and he buttons and zips, puts on a white undershirt
that was on the floor. His steel-toe boots.

"Where you want to go, Omi Ruth?"

"Chalkers pool hall," I say, as if I go there every day of the week.

Vaughn shakes his head and laughs again. "Closed on Sunday morning. This ain't exactly prime time for getting into trouble." Smiles bigger now. "And don't try to tell me you're not here for trouble." He sweeps over to me with that hand-curve starting at my waist and sliding up to my armpit, thumb just edging my chest, and he kisses me without asking. I taste the sleep on his tongue. I feel all four walls.

"I've got an idea though," he says, looking down at me as if my dress isn't really there. "There's a place we can go." I hear something in his voice that scares me, that makes me change my mind and touch my lips that are too red. But we're out the door, he's taken my hand. In my head I'm saying, I'm cruel. I'm cruel.

Vaughn drives us through downtown in minutes, past the diner, past the cemetery. He cuts through the farms down straight county roads I don't recognize. He flies, shifts up, flies faster, like he's trying to prove something. In the muscle car's side mirror, I watch the exhaust pipe belch black smoke behind us. Past the outer edge of Dunlap, farther than I've flown in months, maybe farther than ever.

He gets bolder the faster he drives, racing some other car we can't see, reaching over to me and touching my chin—smiling—my neck, my pieced-out curls. Just once he slips his hand between my legs, too quickly for me to catch him. Dress thin, underwear thin between his skin and me. Rows of cornstalks tremor where their summer silks have been, and there's nothing else in the world, just my own self waking to his own self, me breathing so fast and rising and rising so the dress might truly disappear and me with it. So fast my shudder comes, like rippling light, a flood, and I sink back into the seat as into water. He whispers my name and rolls his eyes to the back of his head and pulls his hand away on his own, like it's electric that will shock my water, like he knows I wouldn't have pushed him away in a million years, not this time, even though a small part of me inside this grown-woman self is sensing a terrible thing coming. He drives even faster, and I think of all the girls he's had, but I don't care, and I don't listen to my fear. I'm the girl he thinks is talented and dressed to kill. I was a limp, weak-stemmed flower, but I'm growing stronger, just so I can get weak again. I finger the miniature dove swinging from the rearview, its sharp pointy wings. I wear a tiara of silver sunflowers, I'm not as ugly as I'd once bitterly thought, and we are far far beyond the edge of what I know about the world.

Vaughn pulls off the road, into the browning rows of corn. Their thick paper leaves rustle in the wind to the sound of our fast breathing. We calm our breath and don't speak. Half a dozen cars and trucks huddle around the base of the radio tower a ways off, hard cobwebs of metal and wire. There's a bonfire going, looking hazy and too angry under afternoon sky. We're parked far enough away that no one has noticed us. I look over at him and remember the night I asked him under his dome light to buy me a headstone with stolen money. He looked slumped over and weary then, coming right off shift, and he looks that way now. Not seventeen, but older, and at once younger, too young to work the heavy machines. Too boyish to look me in my hungry eyes. He's lost, I think then, without knowing his daddy, and I guess I'm lost, too, together but not together. Side by side, but nowhere. We're glued to the vinyl bench seat of nowhere, our bodies so awake they hurt.

"Who are they?" I ask about the kids around the tower.

He exhales, looking relieved at the sound of my voice. "Trouble," his old smile coming back, his dangerous face. He unlatches his door, about to get out, and I'm trapped by the tall corn on my side so I slide over to follow, but he stops and I'm suddenly on top of him, in his lap. His arms wrap me around and I feel him in my hair, laughing a little and breathing in the mint-tea smell of the pomade. I can feel the front of his pants raised up underneath me. We're still still, not breathing at all now.

What will he do? What have I done? The scared part of me tries to wriggle free but he keeps me on top of him, he is stronger, and I can tell he's looking to the right, toward the dying corn where he could get me alone and no one would hear a thing. But he just looks and holds me still, he doesn't move, and I grow bolder. I slowly take one of his arms and unwind it. I take his hand that has the callus; I slide it under my dress skirt. I'm cruel Omi Ruth Wincott who is lost and old and about to be born. I guide his fingers like I have guided my North's, only Vaughn's fingers quiver, they pulse. I think about all the other girls but I think I was wrong about what they did, for he is shaking. I close my eyes and rub his fingertips over my soft wet underwear, picturing tiny butterflies though I know they're plain white. I let go and his fingers live and move, they slide themselves under the cloth, into the tender valleys, and then deeper down, deeper till he is up inside me—oh—I grip his other hard arm, so so wide open that my shudder can't come and its not-coming is me on the trapeze about to fall, back and forth through the air, the motion of Vaughn's tender hand, about to fall, about to, and then he stifles a small cry, his own—I feel, at once, the wet at the front of his pants underneath me. Then I am off him and over nearer the corn. His head is back and rolled like he's dead, but then he opens his eyes. I watch his throat swallow. He reaches somewhere behind the seat and grabs a work shirt, puts it on, and snaps it. It's long enough to cover his front. He wipes his eyes, and I look into the neat, silent corn rows. The stalks witnesses to how sad and lovely we suddenly are, how silent, just like them.

Till I finally speak. "I don't know where I am."

"Just one county over, Naomi." His voice cracks when he says my full name. "Not that far. But you'll like this." He nods, runs his fingers through his hair. He's sweating though it's cold. "Just wait till you see this." He's trying to find words to say, to prove something like when he was racing invisible cars. Am I cruel? Am I beautiful out here, out of Elkhart County? I think about my home ec classes from last spring; I try to figure out what it is we've done.

A huge flame shoots up over the bonfire by the tower. Shouts and whooping.

"Just wait, Omi. These Amish fuckers'll do all kinds of shit." Vaughn sits in a way that broadens his shoulders. "Odell told me about this place."

Amish. I think Spencer Frye and feel a stab. "Maybe we should leave, Vaughn." I look for a horse and buggy but see none.

"Nah, come on, Omi. I said I'd show you trouble. Isn't that what you wanted?"

Isn't that what I wanted? Didn't I want to show Tracie all that I know? All the many things?

"It's like these kids just broke out of prison," he says. "They're good little Amish boys till they turn sixteen, then all hell breaks loose. Odell says they drink *him* under the table. And there's girls, too. Not looking as pretty as you though." He smiles, and I see he wants to get out. It's not just to please me. He's after trouble, too. He has been too tender with me.

I think of Spencer on rumspringa, his rock-band T-shirt. The kinds of things maybe he has done.

"Come on, Omi. Then I'll take you home, or wherever you want. I'll take you anyplace you want." He touches my shoulder, his hand stiffer now. He unlatches the door. I slide over like before, but this time we both get out, and our legs are weak. It's hard for us to stand, which makes Vaughn laugh and tug his shirt down farther over his pants.

I see a boy hanging on the chain-link fence that boxes in the tower. He's got a big jug; I watch him jerk it forward to send a stream of liquid into the fire so it roars up again.

"Crazy kid's got gasoline," Vaughn says. The cool air climbs up my arms and under my polka-dotted dress. I bat the air away, something feels very wrong, I try to picture Solomon's Porch and its dirty white paint and familiar rooms, I hear whooping and flame. We walk closer until they notice us, ten boys or so and a few girls that surprise me with their white caps and plain Amish dresses. "Told you there's girls," he says. One of them flashes a big smile and shouts and raises a can she drinks from and leans into the girl beside her. Everybody takes a drink like she does, giving off a chorus of shouts that worry me rigid. I cling to Vaughn.

Then I see him.

Spencer out at the edge, tossing his hair from his eyes. White sneakers. I see him at the same time I see the horse and buggy on the other end of the tower's fence, almost hidden in the corn. He meets my eyes then looks at my party dress, looks at Vaughn then looks at the ground. He holds one of the beer cans, too. Vaughn pulls me toward the fire, and a blond-haired boy holds out two beers to us.

"I thought you might be the authorities," the blond boy says in a voice formal like Spencer's, but with his tongue thick. "We cannot have them around. This is somebody's private land." He laughs.

"Here's your trouble," Vaughn whispers to me, no longer shy or slow or sweet. I see something in him that makes him more like Odell. I say no to the beer, but he says he won't mind drinking both.

The day is warmer here in the sun, but I feel a deep chill. Vaughn does a fast drinking contest with the blond boy, and I wander over where the three girls stand in a huddle, cans dangling between their fingers like big cheap charms. I'm closer to Spencer now, but he turns his back to break off dried ears of corn that weren't harvested. He throws them into the fire, which warms my arm closest to it. Goosebumps, as if my skin's trying to feel more and more of the heat.

"Would you like a jacket?" a girl asks me, and I take the denim jacket that reminds me of Wood's. I see that she wears plain clothes but has pierced her ears and wears sneakers with pink laces.

We all stand a long time near the radio tower in the clearing of corn. I don't learn anyone's name. Vaughn keeps going farther into the cornfield with the blond boy to find more dried ears to toss onto the fire. The same boy from before keeps climbing the chain-link fence to spray a stream of gasoline into the flames, more gas each time, from a bottomless jug. He must think he climbs the high radio tower instead of just the fence because he puts his hand to his mouth and hollers, "I see the whole world from up here!"

Spencer doesn't look at me much. He stays in a group of three other quiet boys, dressed the same as he is. They squat and tip each other over, so easily, they're so drunk. I remember that it's my birthday and that there's a cake. It's late afternoon, it's dusk. I remember the horrible things I said to Tracie. I remember she held her belly holding Baby Jax like she felt some pain.

One boy shoves another too hard, and the toppled boy's head hits the fence.

"Shit!" the boy says, pulling a hand from his head starting to bleed. "Shit, you! How's come—you, shit!" He slurs all his words and drops his beer. "You shit!" he yells again and runs back at the other till they're both down in the corn and the cornstalks crackle and shake. A couple other boys jump on, yelling, "Fight, fight," and I look for Vaughn but he's disappeared deep into the field again, after the dried-out ears.

Then I hear a siren, not too far away, coming from the direction we came from.

"They're coming!" somebody yells, and kids begin to run every which way into the corn.

"Spencer!" I shout, but where is he? He must be with the fighting boys in the dirt, but how could he be?

It's happening fast but in slow motion too, the sirens getting so close they're breaking into my head, and the same boy climbs the chain-link fence again, pushing away the pink-laces girl who tries to stop him. Another boy with Amish suspenders over his T-shirt runs over to stop him, too, saying "We need to go," but the climber knocks him back with the jug, sloshing out some gas onto the boy's suspenders and shirt and skin. He's on the ground, the other is in the sky, way on top of the radio tower where he sees the whole wide world that he sprinkles again with his endless supply of gasoline—"Stop!" the girl screams—but the gas rains down in a line from the fire to the boy on the ground and flames lick out, so eager, toward the dirt and toward the boy. He catches fire.

He is screaming, burning alive, this boy is wild in motion and sound, rolling this way, that way into the ragged corn. Vaughn is nowhere, we are all side by side but nowhere. Someone is honking a horn to draw the sirens closer—to guide the police to the boy who burns. Spencer's arms suddenly surround me, covering my face and burying me deep into his chest to hear only his heartbeats, horribly loud ones. It's deafening, it's like he is in there pounding to get out, but the image of burning, the jug of gasoline, I can't shake it—I must be trying to shake it, for he tries to hold my head still, but I break free, I run, right into the cornstalks rough and sharp and punishing. I run and run and they scrape my legs, I hear the sirens reach the clearing, I hear someone running behind me, Spencer Frye, saying "Wait, Naomi, wait, wait," but I'm lost in a maze of corn and soon he's so far away, his voice is a tiny pinpoint of sound. I'm crying and the pictures come on me without mercy, the boy ablaze and Vaughn with his head rolled back and Spencer seeing my body's full shudder in my eyes, every pluck of flower in his mother's kitchen garden before dawn, flowers named *Naomi*, named *Ruth*, the sad slow sweetness of boys swallowed up by fire and snakes, those tattooed fangs chewing up Odell's hard arm. Not allowed sweetness anymore. Only on radio, you can be sweet on radio, but once your shy body makes its way out into the world, it will harden and burn and you'll be nothing but mean.

I don't know where I am. The corn lets me go, and it's a paved road, straight. My sides ache, but I run the county road with the *click click* of my red shoes till I take them off and throw them far. The denim jacket, too, for it smells of smoke and something more. It's dark now, my breath all jagged. Headlights, but I keep running, for it might be Vaughn and I can't have him near me. Great pouring of light all around and the vehicle slows, stops, and chugs on without moving, some-where behind me. The driver gets out.

"Omi Ruth!" It's her. "Omi Ruth, you come here! You hear me?"

I turn. Tracie's a shadow next to the headlights that pin me to the air. Her hand on her belly, I can see that. It's Morse's truck chugging.

"I been down every damn road in this state," she yells. "Now you come here. Where you running to?"

I can't move, my feet feel sliced.

"You still mad?" she asks.

I shake my head no, my whole body no. The polka-dotted skirt flares.

"Come here," she says. "It's no party without the birthday girl. Couple presents waiting for you."

I fly to her, so fast I don't feel my cut-up feet, and she catches me.

"You had me scared sick, girl. Don't you ever do that again."

"Oh, Tracie, I'm cruel," I say.

"Hush now. You didn't mean nothing by it. I know, and me neither."

"I'm cruel," I say again, "I'm cruel, I'm cruel," so softly into her neck till my lips move without sound. She strokes and strokes my hair, starts taking out my silver sunflower barrettes—like I'm lying under our Big Top on my old gingham bed spread, and not standing beside Morse's truck on some far-off county road, halfway to nowhere and barefoot.

ABOUT THE AUTHOR

Jessie van Eerden holds an MFA in nonfiction writing from the University of Iowa. Her debut novel *Glorybound* (Word-Farm) was awarded *ForeWord Reviews'* 2012 Editor's Choice Fiction Prize. Her essays, short stories, and poems have appeared in *The Oxford American, Bellingham Review, Rock & Sling, Memorious, The Literary Review,* and other publications. Her essays have been selected for inclusion in *Best American Spiritual Writing, The River Teeth Reader, Red Holler: An Anthology of Contemporary Appalachian Literature,* and *Walk Till the Dogs Get Mean: Meditations on the Forbidden from Contemporary Appalachia.* Jessie lives in West Virginia where she directs the low-residency MFA writing program at West Virginia Wesleyan College.

CPSIA information can be obtained
at www.ICGtesting.com
Printed in the USA
FFOW05n0543030316

9 781943 665082